THE TOY CUPBOARD

THE TOY CUPBOARD

Lee Jordan

Walker and Company
New York

All the characters and events portrayed in this work are fictitious.

First published in the United States of America in 1990
by Walker Publishing Company, Inc.

Published simultaneously in Canada by Thomas Allen & Son
Canada, Limited, Markham, Ontario

Library of Congress Cataloging-in-Publication Data

Jordan, Lee.
The toy cupboard / Lee Jordan.
ISBN 0-8027-5775-8
I. Title.
PR6060.06254T69   1990
823'.914—dc20   90-12460
CIP

Printed in the United States of America

2   4   6   8   10   9   7   5   3   1

1

'Littlemissmuffet . . . satona . . . ona . . .'
'Tuffet.'
'Tuffet.'
'Go on.'
'Eatinghercurdsand . . . '
'Whey.'
'Whey.'
'Go on.'
'I don't want to.'
'Go on or you know what'll happen! There came . . .'
'Therecameabigspider . . .'
'And?'
'Andsatdownbesideher . . .'
'No! He didn't sit down! What did he do?'
'He shot him. With a gun.'
'Who's him? You don't call him that.'
'I don't want to.'
'You *have* to! Say it!'
'Daddy.'
'That's right. Daddy. And who's Miss Muffet?'
'I don't know.'
'I'm sick of you! I'm going to—'
'No!'
'Well then, say it!'
'The lady.'
'What lady?'
'The lady with . . . with daddy '

He shot her, didn't he? The big spider shot her too.'
Yes. The big spider.'
You better remember.'
But afterwards she had always tried to forget.

2

Jo Townsend had been watching the man watch her. She had been aware of him for the past hour. He was making a big deal about taking pictures, aiming the 35mm compact in every direction except at her stall, but each time she glanced in his direction he seemed to be looking at her.

It was eleven o'clock on a cold, misty, Sunday morning at Camden Lock Market in North London and the crowds were at their thickest. The noise was tremendous. She watched the man as he walked slowly among the stalls. He was dressed in a red and white parka and he stopped at a counter with a display of Nazi insignia. He picked up an SS badge, looked at it, replaced it; lifted a Panzer officer's cap, looked at it, replaced it.

The lines of stalls stretched into the distance beyond him. Jo's stall was at the lockside near a decrepit boat that was permanently moored and carried a display of old movie stars' photographs in wooden frames. There was Gary Cooper in his *High Noon* pose, John Garfield, Barbara Stanwyck, June Allyson, Donna Reed, Guy Madison, Kim Novak in a shot from *Vertigo*, and dozens more.

The stall next to Jo's was badges: every lapel badge there ever was from KEEP THE POPE OFF THE MOON to BASH A GRANNY TODAY.

The man in the red and white parka was just above medium height but the padded jacket made him look solid. He had straight black hair and olive skin. She

7

couldn't place his nationality but he looked 'foreign' and yet not an obvious tourist.

He took a picture of the rusty old narrowboat floating in the scummy green water surrounded by empty cigarette packs and styrofoam cups. Click, click, she thought, that's one for the holiday album. She could imagine him pulling it out at the office in wherever and telling everyone that this was Britain in the 1980s: all rust and rubbish. And she had to admit that if you took this part of Camden Town as representative – with its filthy streets and ripe graffiti – then that's exactly what it was. You could smell the hash in the air.

She stamped up and down in her Ugg boots and warmed her fingers at her mouth.

A family came between her and the happy snapper: husband, wife and boy with thick glasses. The boy picked up a lapel badge and looked at it.

'I pump New York,' he said.

'It's "love",' his mother said. 'The heart means love. "I love New York".'

'The heart's a pump,' the boy said. He picked up several other badges and dropped them one by one on the counter. 'I pump my Mini. I pump Australia. I pump the Beatles. I—'

'Jeffrey!'

'I *pump* windsurfing. I pump—'

'*Jeffrey!*'

'I pump New Zealand lamb. I pump sausages. I pump—'

'For Christ's sake I'll pump you in a minute!' his father said, dragging him away.

Jo looked for the man in the parka but he seemed to have vanished. She shivered, partly from the cold but also from a sense of unease. Had he been watching her? Or was it her imagination? There had been another man yesterday, the one in the hat with the feather. She thought he'd been watching her, too. 'I'm irresistible,' she told herself. 'Everyone's trying to get their hands on me.' It was meant to cheer her up on this bleak Sunday morning and it did – a bit. Then she thought of the empty flat and wished Michael was back.

Her sister, Flora, arrived with cups of hot chicken soup. 'Sell anything?'

'Two graters and that sieve with the hole in it. The one Michael picked up in Leeds.'

Flora straightened the display of Victorian kitchenware on the counter. She was always straightening things. Jo placed a Viennese coffee grinder circa 1927 at the front of the stall. It wasn't Victorian but, as Michael said, who the hell would know the difference?

'Not that one!' Flora said sharply. 'I told you not that one! It's sold!'

'Sorry.'

'I told you before about these. You're grown-up, for God's sake. I shouldn't have to remind you all the time.' She took the coffee grinder and put it in her capacious brown shopping bag.

It would have been difficult to guess that these two were sisters. Jo was small and golden, and even with her short brown hair tucked under an unflattering beanie she looked like a stunning eighteen-year-old. Flora was half a head taller, dark and with a thin sharply-etched face. She was nine years older than Jo. Once, before she met her first husband, she had been a model. It showed. She still dressed with flair and when she was made-up men turned to look at her rakish body, all angles and shadows.

'There's something about her that attracts attention,' Michael had once said to Jo.

'Didn't mean to snap,' Flora said after a moment.

9

'It's okay. My fault, my mind was somewhere else.'

She had just seen the man in the red and white parka. He was standing on a box about twenty feet away, half hidden by the canvas top of a stall. This time he was taking a picture of the two of them.

3

Unlike the cold mist of London, the Mediterranean, on that Sunday morning, was blue and gold. A mistral had been blowing for two days bringing dry cold air down the Rhône Valley but now it had dropped, the sun shone and the air was warm enough to sit out and take a pastis before lunch. And nowhere was it warmer or sunnier than Marseilles.

This was just as well, for a great many things were going on along the coast: the Prix du Midi cycle race was starting at the Old Port of Marseilles and circling through Toulon and Hyères, into the lonely Forêt des Maures before finishing again in Marseilles; there was a Fête de Ballon with balloonists competing from as far away as Austria; Nice football club was at home to Montpellier; there was a major *boules* tournament at Antibes, and there were hill-climbs and go-karting and a powerboat race from Cannes to St Tropez and back – all in all a vigorous winter Sunday.

But in the Baumettes prison Sundays were not like that. In the front office, Hector Blagny, one of the duty officers, finished cutting his fingernails, put the clippers away in his drawer and pulled the Day Book towards him.

Not all screws liked Sunday duty, but he didn't mind. He was in his forties, bald, overweight – and oversexed. Or that's what Maria said. She was half Italian and worked in a restaurant in Bandol. That way they both had Mondays off and could spend the day in bed together. She was very religious, or said she was. It didn't stop her wanting it all the time though. Some Mondays he was so tired by evening he could hardly stand.

Often when he was banging away he would look up and see the Blessed Virgin staring down at him from a wall niche. He had complained it was enough to put anyone off his stroke but Maria said She had to stay.

At the desk behind him, Laborde was reading *France Dimanche*. He was fifteen years younger than Blagny, thin and hollow-chested, dark, like a Corsican. He talked a lot about all the women he had had but Blagny doubted his tales. His experience was that talkers were not doers. Now Laborde said, 'You think Princess Di's got a lover?'

'What?'

Laborde flicked the newspaper. 'Princess Di. It says she's got a lover. She's going to leave that Prince of Wales. It says he's too old for her. It's true. He's more like her father.'

Blagny felt aggrieved.

'He's too old for discos,' Laborde continued. 'It says they never go out to nightclubs.'

'Nightclubs! Who the hell wants to go to nightclubs? Listen, you think he's too old to do it? Let me tell you, sonny—'

The door of the office opened and a man entered. He was very big, with a big head and big hands. He was in his late fifties but looked older, for his skin was sallow and waxy. He walked with a kind of shuffle and his head seemed too heavy for his neck, drawing him forward into a stoop.

Blagny stared at him for a few moments, his eyes widening, as though he were seeing a ghost. 'Drac?' he said. 'Is it you?'

The big man stared at him.

Blagny burst out laughing. 'Have you seen yourself?' He turned, 'Laborde, you fancy yourself as a ladies' man, tell

12

me the date of that suit. Narrow lapels, sloping shoulders, two buttons.'

'How the hell should I know?' Laborde said.

'My first suit looked like that,' Blagny said. 'God how I loved it.'

Blagny opened the Day Book and looked at an entry. 'The date's the same.'

'What date?' Laborde said, confused.

'The date of the suit, idiot. 1968.' Then to Drac, 'You bought it for the trial?'

Drac said nothing. He reminded Blagny of an artist's impression he had once seen of the Minotaur: the gross head and shoulders, the small, hidden eyes. There had been a time when he would never have laughed at Marcel Drac. But that time had long since passed.

'Well, well,' he continued. 'So you leave us today. Can't we change your mind?' To Laborde, 'You wouldn't think he was a killer, would you? And a famous one! Why don't you tell Laborde what you did, Drac? Impress him. Young people don't impress easily these days.'

Drac lowered his head a fraction further. Don't mix it, he told himself. Let the bastard have his say. Don't screw-up now or they'll find some way of stopping you.

'Tell him what you did, Marcel.'

'Forget it,' Laborde said. 'If he's going today I'll get his things.'

'No, no,' Blagny said. 'I want you to hear. We've got an aristo here. I mean as killers go. First he kills the Englishman and then the woman. Were you married to her, Marcel? I can't remember. It doesn't matter. She was a whore, anyway. Used to work the casino at Cassis. Isn't that so?'

Briefly a vision of Yvette flashed into Drac's mind. It was mention of the casino that did it. He had successfully obliterated all thought of her for twenty years and he didn't want to start thinking about her just yet. Once he

13

was home it would be all right. But not here, not now.

'I remember the trial well,' Blagny was saying. 'Same time as I bought my suit. It was in the Paris papers too, not just the locals. The big-time. Love nest murder, *crime passionel*, call it what you like, but there was a difference: in this case the victim was a *rosbif*. You like the English, Laborde?'

'Not much. But not enough to kill them.'

'Same with me. But not Marcel. Not when the *rosbif* and his woman are having it off. You forgotten all about that kind of thing, Drac? Officer Laborde thinks a man's too old at thirty.'

Drac's head moved lower. It was a survival posture he had learned years before. Drop the head, drop the eyes, look down at the carpet. That way you didn't make anyone angry.

'You know, Drac,' Blagny continued, 'I'm surprised you survived. Twenty years is a long time.' He turned to Laborde. 'If I had been the judge he would have got the . . .' He made a cutting motion across his throat.

'For killing someone who was making it with his woman?' Laborde said. 'Never!'

'No, no. You don't get that for killing your wife's lover. Not even if he is a *rosbif*. No, that was only five years. The rest was for a prison officer. One of us. It was just after I came here. Hit the man from behind and broke his neck. He was strong in those days. Not like this relic you see here! Pathetic! He hasn't even got the brains to be damaged by prison. But we'll see you again, Drac. You'll never get on out there.' Blagny paused. His anger had momentarily caused him to lose his breath. After a few seconds he pulled himself together. 'All right, Laborde. Get his things and let's get him out of here.'

4

The mist was thickening over London and the day was dying. It was barely mid-afternoon but the street lights were on and the crowds in Camden Lock Market were thinning fast. Some traders had already packed up and gone.

At the height of trading the place was dressed up by colour, interest and people, but now it was beginning to show its wretchedness.

It occupied a series of derelict warehouses on the Grand Union Canal. Once, a hundred years ago, the word 'grand' might have had some meaning, not now. Here the canal was foetid and unloved.

It was nineteenth-century London, a place of shadows and dirt, where Mayhew might have come to interview prostitutes and footpads, where Dickens might have placed Fagin and the child criminals.

Jo Townsend was also preparing to go. Flora had already departed, and she had been left to pack up. She used a series of tea chests and old holdalls for her goods and after she had filled them she began to loosen the metal rods which acted as a framework on which the stall's protective canvas was hung.

When she had started as a market trader more than a year before she had taken ages to erect and dismantle the stall, now it was second nature.

As she worked she kept an eye out for the man in the red and white parka but he was nowhere to be seen.

Perhaps she had imagined his interest, perhaps she had imagined the man with the feather in his hat too. Perhaps it was Camden Lock itself which created the backdrop for such thoughts.

It was as well she had not told Flora of her fears. Flora was dismissive of such weaknesses. Jo remembered that even as a child when she had scraped a knee, or been terrified of a shadow in her room at night, her sister would say, 'You always make fusses. You make more fuss than anyone I know.'

Flora never made fusses. That was one of her strengths. 'A tough cookie' Mike had called her. Well, you had to be tough in the fashion world. When Flora was one of the top models in England, Jo had been in her mid-teens and old enough to observe the fringe of that world, dominated by money, sex, powerful men. You *had* to be tough to deal with it.

But if she was mistaken about the man in the red and white parka then she was losing her touch, Jo thought. Women were supposed to know when men were interested in them – wasn't that what made the world go round?

She thought: I'll drink to that. Where would we be without them? And instantly she felt a sense of guilt. Women shouldn't be dependent on that sort of sexist reaction.

She had spent much of her youth marching. She had marched against nuclear bombs and nuclear power; she had marched for Women's Liberation, and Gay Rights, and Save the Albert Hall; she had marched for nurses, and Russian Jews, and Palestinians, for pensioners and for the right to work and for Free Kurds – even though at the time she wasn't sure whether it was a place or something to eat.

This had been when she was living with Peter. She remembered him with fondness. Dear, earnest, committed and caring Peter. They had lived together in a squat in Battersea with a group of militants so extreme they considered Trotskyites a bunch of right-wing pansies. She used to go and see her sister three or four times a week just to have a bath.

Eventually they broke up and Peter disappeared into a commune in Scotland where they kept their own sheep, spun the wool and made their own hairy clothing. They 'shared' each other so that the children had multiple parents in an extended family.

After Peter, she had tried marching by herself but it wasn't the same. Then she had gone to Greenham Common to demonstrate outside the US missile base. If Peter had been a girl he would have loved the campfires and sleeping rough. Jo hadn't much cared for the way determined ladies kept trying to get into her sleeping bag. The trouble was, as Peter had said, she just wasn't the stuff of political activists.

She finished folding the canvas and thought, wouldn't it be nice if Mike was back when she got home and they could have a drink together.

Often when he was away on a buying trip she would go round to Flora's for supper on a Sunday, but tonight Flora had things to do, fish to fry, Mr Whoozit to entertain.

So she would go home to Pimlico and have a lovely evening with the lovely telly and get into her lovely big double bed – all by her lovely self. That seemed to be the norm these days. What a bloody waste.

'Jo!' She looked up. Harry Evans was standing in front of the stall. 'Look what Harry's got!' He was holding a bottle of Bacardi, a litre of Coke and two glasses. 'Am I the answer to a maiden's prayer?'

'Harry, I love you.'

He poured the drinks and gave her one. '*Salud y pesetas!*' he said.

'Cheers.'

Harry had a stall along the row from hers. He sold

17

anything to do with motor-bikes – badges, books, photographs, leathers, boots, gloves, gauntlets, Biggles flying helmets, goggles. He was in his late forties or early fifties and was the oldest hippy in the market.

Many times Jo had seen him arrive on his reconditioned Harley, huge, like something out of Hell's Angels in all his gear. But as each layer was stripped off he became smaller and smaller until it wasn't King Kong standing there, but little Harry Evans from Whitechapel. His shoulder-length hair was grey, his beard was grey, and he wore wire granny-glasses. Occasionally, after a few drinks, he might come on strong and Jo would have to fend him off, but right now, she decided, he was solid gold.

They had another drink and talked for a while, lying to each other, as all stall holders did, about the day's selling, then he said, 'You on your ace? Where's Mike? He's never here these days.'

'He's on a buying trip in Scotland.'

'Scotland, at this time of year! Jesus! And Flora?'

'She left about an hour ago.'

'Shit! I told her I'd see her.'

'When?'

'I didn't say a time.'

'She got cold.'

'Didn't she leave nothing then?'

'What sort of thing?'

'A present for an old geezer.' He looked over his shoulder as though Flora or the old geezer might have been behind him. 'She says she's got something. Perfect present.'

'She didn't tell me.'

He drained his glass and screwed the tops back on the two bottles. Suddenly he was in a hurry.

'She went home,' Jo said. 'It's not far.'

'I know. Okay. Thanks.'

18

He waited for her to drain her glass and took it from her. 'See you,' he said.

She watched him walk away and disappear into the darkness. It was then she realised that in this part of the large complicated market area she was by herself.

A wind had come up, causing the mist to swirl about the lamps. Pieces of paper skittered across the ground.

She had a sudden urge to call Harry, to run after him, but then she heard the roar of the Harley as he drove off through the large double exit gates that led into Chalk Farm Road. Out there were cars and people and shops, ordinary things. That was what she wanted.

She moved fast. Running and walking, she carried the tea chests and the holdalls to her van and dumped them in. It took three trips and she had to force herself back into the market each time.

This is ridiculous, she thought. But, just as a child will conjure up terrors in a darkened room, so she saw every shadowy corner as a place where something, a man, an animal, anything – might be hiding.

She got into the van, closed the door and locked it. She let out a sigh of relief. That was that. She drove out of the market and the first thing she saw was an ordinary red double-decker bus with ordinary people sitting in it. It was a powerfully reassuring symbol. She smiled and then she raised her hand and waved at a middle-aged lady in the bus who pretended not to see her.

But Jo *was* seen by the man who'd been wearing the red and white parka. He wasn't wearing it now because he was sitting in his car waiting for her. She turned left out of the gates and he followed her through the back streets of Chalk Farm and across the Edgware Road. She took a series of short cuts, then drove into the park. It was easy to follow her for she was driving a VW microbus. He was in a silver-grey Saab.

She had no idea she was being followed. Having left

the market she had also left her fears. The VW was her territory. She had bought it with her own money and in it she felt safe. She pushed in a cassette of Pink Floyd and sang with them through Kensington and Chelsea and finally pulled up outside a house in Pimlico.

The Saab parked half a block away. The driver's name was Roger Maillet. And Jo was right. He *had* been watching her in the market. Now he watched her get out of the VW and disappear into a house. He lit a Gitane, turned on the radio softly, and settled down to wait.

It was a small house, built in the nineteen-fifties on a bombed site. On the ground floor was a kitchen/dining-room, the sitting-room was on the first floor and there were two bedrooms on the second. Jo thought it was terrific. Mike thought it was piddling: his word. Sometimes, when he was home, he would drive her around Hampstead in his white BMW and point out the sort of house he wanted and which they were going to have one day. They started at three-quarters of a million.

'So what?' he said.

'We'll have to sell an awful lot of coffee grinders.'

'Think big.'

But for an out-of-work actress and an antique dealer she still thought the Pimlico house was terrific. Sometimes she wondered how they had managed even that.

Of course, once they had a couple of kids they'd need a bigger place. That's if they ever did. Mike always changed the subject if she brought it up, and latterly it had irritated him.

She flicked on the hall lights, dropped her keys on the table, and ran up the stairs. Halfway up she smelled cigarette smoke.

'Mike!' She ran towards the drawing-room door. 'Mike, you bastard! Why didn't you let—'

She flung open the door.

'—me know!'

The room was in darkness but she could see his seated silhouette against the windows. She put on the light. A man was certainly sitting in one of her chairs, but it wasn't Mike.

He was thirtyish, tall and well built, with long dark sideburns. He was wearing an expensive camel-hair topcoat. She particularly noticed his hat, a natty Tyrolean job with a pheasant's feather at the side.

And she had just time to notice something else: the room was in chaos. The sofa had been overturned. Paintings and lithographs had been taken down from the walls. The lamps had been knocked over and so had a beautiful Hepplewhite chair which Mike had found in a Yorkshire attic and for which he had paid a pittance.

She noticed all this in a matter of seconds, about as long as it took the man to rise from his chair and grab her arm. His other hand caught her throat. She felt herself being propelled backwards. She tried to scream but the fingers tightened. She knew there something called a hyoid bone in the neck and that it was fragile and if it broke that was the finish. So she stopped trying to scream.

'So . . . This is besser,' the man said, relaxing his grip slightly. 'You shout, I kill you. Yes?'

'Please . . . ' It was no more than a croak.

He gripped her arm, spun her round, and pushed. His strength was amazing. She flew across the room, unable to control her movements. She hit an overturned chair, and then cannoned into the wall with her shoulder. She moaned with pain.

She looked up and he was standing over her. His face was impassive. If there was any expression at all, it was one of mild interest.

'Where is Mick?' he said.

'Mick?'

He caught her by her hair, lifted her, and spun her

21

round again: and again she was out of control, arms and legs flapping, body gyrating. This time she ended up half under the sofa.

She saw his shoes. For a terrible moment she thought he was going to kick her and she twisted herself into a ball, covering her breasts with her elbows.

Instead he sat on the sofa, bent down, and took her face in his hand. He squeezed her cheeks until she felt her teeth begin to cut into her flesh.

'Where is Mick?'

It was the way he said it that had confused her. He had an Austrian accent and he pronounced it 'Meek'.

'Michael,' she said, tasting blood in her mouth.

'Mick.'

'Mike. But there's some mistake.'

'Where is he?'

'Look, I—'

Quite casually, he slapped her face. He had a gold signet ring on the fourth finger of his right hand and she felt it crack against the bone of her eyebrow.

'Where is he?' His voice was still soft.

'I don't know wh—'

He hit her again.

'For God's *sake*! I don't *know*. You've been watching me! You know he's not around!'

She tried to get up but he pushed her down with his foot. She was crying now, in anger and fear and pain, and the tears were running down to mix with the mucous from her nose. She sniffed and used her sleeve as though she were a child again.

'Please . . .' she said. 'Whatever it is, you've got the wrong people. Wrong address. Wrong everything.'

He rose. 'I do not believe so.' He brushed fastidiously at his coat then touched her leg with the toe of a highly polished crocodile-skin shoe. 'You give a message to Mick. You tell him Willi was here. But no

22

police, yes? You go to the police we kill Mick – and you too.' He moved to the doorway and raised his hat. He was wearing a brown toupee which had shifted to one side of his bald head. He was unaware of this and gave a small formal bow. '*Wiedersehen*,' he said.

5

'Hey! Hey, wake up!'

Marcel Drac came out of sleep with his arms up round his head, half expecting to feel a blow. Hands were on his collar, shaking him.

Then he knew it wasn't a dream. He could hear the big diesels thumping away, smell the dust and fumes. He was in a bus. The driver was shaking him.

'La Motte,' the driver said.

Drac gathered himself. His head was still pounding from the pastis he'd had at lunchtime. Pastis, then cognac. Not a good mix. But what the hell? You get out of prison, you celebrate the best way you know how.

He nodded to the driver, picked up his battered suitcase and walked down the aisle. There were half a dozen passengers. He could see them looking at him as though he came from another world. It must be the suit, he thought. Well, to hell with them. The material was as good as new. He'd only worn it in the courtroom. He'd wear it whatever people thought. He dropped down on to the road and the bus accelerated away.

For the first time in nearly twenty years he was quite alone and for a moment he felt a rising sense of panic.

He looked about him. The bus had dropped him on a long straight and what cars there were passed him at speed.

The afternoon sun was dropping behind the Col du Canadel and the shadows were long. The air had a greyish quality and he could feel the cold beginning to flow across the ground. He picked up his case and crossed the road. On his left was the little airfield with a couple of light planes parked at the far end. It hadn't changed. That was something.

Parts of the coast had been like looking at an alien landscape. America maybe. The new blocks of apartments were eight, ten, fifteen storeys high. There had been nothing there when he had gone up, just umbrella pines and scrub. But in this little backwater, nothing seemed to have changed. He'd have a look at La Motte tomorrow, but certainly everything here was the same.

The Route du Canadel left the main Hyères–Cogolin road and wound into low hills. It was bordered by cork oaks and vineyards. At this time of year the vines had been pruned back almost to the ground.

The road surface was rutted and neglected. No one of any importance lived up this road, maybe that's why they didn't keep it up to scratch. Apart from the *rosbif*'s house and his own cottage there were only a few holiday villas owned by foreigners. They would be closed for the winter. If the General lived up this road things would have been different. But he had to remind himself that de Gaulle had been dead for a long time.

Marseilles had changed too. He had never known the city well, but had there always been so many blacks? You expect them in prison, but in the streets? That's not what he'd fought for and been wounded for. He'd fought to keep France white. That's what the General had wanted, or had said he wanted. Then he'd changed his mind overnight. And suddenly it had been Algeria for the Algerians.

His house was three kilometres from the main road and the suitcase was heavy. He wished his head would clear. Or maybe not. Maybe it would be better to go home drunk.

He sat down at the edge of the road, opened the case and drew out the bottle of anisette the tart had sold him. It had a Spanish label. He opened it and took a long swallow. Not bad. The taste reminded him of the arrack he used to drink in Oran. Jesus, but that was bad stuff. He remembered a corporal in his unit who had drunk a bottle in less than half an hour and had died the following day.

Well, he wasn't going to do that. He had other things to do with his life. It was a new life and today was only his first day. He was one day old.

He had said that to the tart in Marseilles but she had looked at him as though he'd lost his marbles. Or maybe it was just apathy. When he hadn't been able to perform she had been angry. She had thought he wasn't going to pay, but money wasn't a problem.

They had put his money away for him each week and he'd drawn what he needed. The rest went to the bank in Cogolin where his army pension and disability allowance had been paid, month in month out, year in year out, for twenty years. All of it in a deposit account. All of it earning interest. If he was careful there was enough to allow him to make his plans carefully. Enough to let him wait. A year. Two years. Ten years. It made no matter. He had enough.

They came out of nowhere. He looked up and they were about twenty yards in front of him, walking down the road from the Col. Two men and a woman and a large black dog. They were walking fast. Gypsies were always like that, he thought. Here one minute, gone the next. The men wore black suits, with white shirts open at the neck. The woman was in a dark dress, a grey cardigan and worn espadrilles. They were brown-skinned, almost like Moroccans, and they looked poor.

They stopped about ten feet from him. One of the men held the dog by a leash. It was a big black mongrel with a high curled tail and a face that had some Rottweiler in it.

'*Bonjour.*' Drac rose slowly to his feet, the bottle in his hand.

'We would like to drink with you,' the man with the dog said.

'A pleasure,' Drac said.

'Unfortunately we do not have anything with us.'

Drac allowed his head to drop a fraction. Shit, he thought, so soon?

'Your dog?'

'Yes.'

'I had a dog like that once. It was called Bizetta.'

The other man laughed. 'Bizetta! That's no name for him. That's a girl's name.'

As though the dog realised they were talking about him he began to growl deep in his throat.

'He could kill you, this dog.'

'Maybe.' Drac said.

'What have you got in the suitcase?' the woman said.

'This and that.'

The dog came at him. He never knew if the man had dropped the leash or the dog had pulled it from his hand but he had been half expecting something of the sort.

Drac moved quickly for a big man. As the dog leapt he swung sideways and hit it in the throat, not hard but enough to cause it to choke for air. It lay in the dust of the road trying to swallow, trying to whine. Drac knelt by it and began to stroke its head.

'How much do you want for him?'

'You want the dog?'

'How much?'

He could see them weighing him up. If they went for him one of them would get hurt, perhaps a broken bone. 'I'll give you a hundred francs.'

The owner laughed.

'What then?'

'You want the dog? You tell me.'

'The hell with you.'

Drac moved away from the dog and seated himself on the suitcase. From his inside pocket he drew a flick knife with a twelve-centimetre blade and began to clean his nails. It was the first thing he had bought after leaving prison. He had bought it in the Quarter. He could have bought anything there, from a .32 Biretta hand-gun to a Kalashnikov assault rifle, and perhaps even a bazooka.

The knife spoke a communal language. The gypsies knew about knives. The situation had changed. An old tramp's suitcase and a bottle of anisette were hardly worth it. What followed now would be ritual. Drac knew it, the gypsies knew it. Fifteen minutes later they had concluded a bargain. A hundred and seventy francs and the bottle of anisette and for that he got the dog and the lead.

He watched them hurry down to the main road and turn in the direction of Cogolin, then he gave his attention to the dog. It was regarding him with hatred mixed with fear. He picked up the end of the lead and the dog snapped at him, its teeth ripping the sleeve of his jacket. This was his 'best' jacket, in fact his only jacket. It annoyed him to see the small three-cornered rip.

He picked up a springy vine branch lying on the roadside and lashed at the dog. It yelped. He jerked the lead and the dog slithered across the ground. He tied the lead to the handle of the suitcase, keeping the case between the two of them. Then, with the stick in his other hand, he began to walk up the road.

'Come,' he said. 'Come, Bizetta!'

Jo sat amid the ruins of her sitting-room, confused and frightened, unwilling, even unable, to take in what had just happened. She was bleeding slightly where the ring had cut her, and her teeth ached. She felt that there were bruises all over her body.

Violence was not uncommon in London, but so far it had only involved other people. Now a man, a foreigner, someone who wore a silly feather in his hat, had beaten her up and vandalised her house. What was even more frightening was that he had seemed so confident, that he knew precisely what he was doing. He had to be wrong, yet he was sure he was right.

Tell Mick Willi was here.

What if he came back? What if there was something he had forgotten to do or say? She ran downstairs and put the heavy chain on the door and locked the two security locks. She hardly ever did that, even though Mike had always told her to. She was usually carrying armloads of stock to or from the van and it was easier to hook her foot around the door and slam it closed on the Yale.

She went back upstairs and phoned Flora. The phone was engaged. She tried again several times, dialling as soon as she got a tone. 'Come on!' she whispered.

She imagined Flora in her flat in Camden Town, lying on her bed perhaps, a glass of vodka in her hands talking to . . . Mr Whoozit.

'Come on!'

Mr Whoozit was a relatively new arrival in Flora's life. Of course there had always been men, as far back as Jo could remember. After her grandmother had died and she had come to live with Flora there had been a whole string of them. Flora had lived in Chelsea then, in a maisonette in Oakley Street – that was when she had plenty of money. She had never been coy. The men had come and gone and if Jo was there they were introduced – Jack or Mark or Guy or whatever. Sometimes they sat around playing tapes and having a drink, sometimes, when she came back from school, she might hear voices coming from

Flora's bedroom. She was fourteen years old then and was expected to mind her own business.

Which she did, because she had always been a bit afraid of Flora. She had told herself it was because Flora had been *in loco parentis*. But one day, one of Flora's men had asked Jo out, and she discovered that her fear had a stronger basis. When Flora had found out, her face became knotted with rage, her eyes like glistening black marbles. She had shaken Jo until her teeth rattled. 'You ever do that to me again and you're finished. You understand! Finished!'

Jo did not quite know what she had meant by 'finished' but did not ask. She was careful after that never to be alone in the same room with Flora's boyfriends.

She dialled again. The line was still engaged. Mr Whoozit was different from the others. He had no name. Flora always referred to him as 'him'. Maybe he was married and she was protecting him. Maybe he was someone they both knew. Maybe Flora was getting ready to marry. Maybe she thought Jo might be competition – which was nonsense. She must always remember that Flora was thirty-five. She was still bloody attractive, Jo thought. But maybe with age you begin to lose confidence in your looks.

'Come on!' She listened for some seconds to the engaged signal.

Anyway, for whatever reason, Flora was being coy about Mr Whoozit. Jo wouldn't hear from her for days at a time. She'd suddenly go into purdah and Jo would know that she and Mr Whoozit were having a fling, either at Flora's flat or somewhere else. It might just be a one-night-stand or it might go on for several days – and usually Flora looked like hell when she re-emerged. Jo dialled again, then slammed the phone down. 'I'm not staying here!' she said aloud, and let herself out of the house.

Roger Maillet in the Saab had watched a man come out of the house. He had been wearing an overcoat and a hat with a feather in it. He wondered if he had seen him before. There was something familiar about the hat. He watched him get into a Ford Sierra and thought of following him, then he told himself it was Mike he was interested in, Mike and Jo. He'd leave the man with the hat for later.

He saw lights go on downstairs. Was she expecting someone else? He settled down to wait. The Third Programme was broadcasting a composition by Harrison Birtwhistle and he listened with mounting indignation. He switched it off and lit another Gitane. Recently he had spent a great deal of time just waiting, but he could not say he was getting used to it.

The house door opened and Jo came out. She was hurrying. She got into the VW and drove off down Sutherland Street, heading for North London. Maillet, in the Saab, followed at a discreet distance.

6

The road up to the house was longer than Drac remembered. The surface grew steadily worse. In the old days they had had a car rally here each winter. He remembered hearing the high engine note of the Renault Alpines and the Matras and the Porches as the drivers came down through the gears, slowing for the sharp left-hander at the little stone bridge. In those days the bridge had been at the bottom of their property. That was before his father had sold the land.

Now the road looked too bad for rallies of any kind. The bush had encroached so that although the sky above the hills was still purplish grey, here, in this tunnel, it was almost night.

Suddenly Fleming's house reared up on the right-hand side. He could see the pink-washed walls and the cedars of Lebanon, the lime tree, and the wall which had been the cause of so much trouble. He felt like climbing it now, as he used to do, and using the old path up into the trees, but decided against it. He knew he was still strong and athletic enough, but he didn't want any trouble. What if someone saw him and reported him to the police?

So he went on up the road, careful not to put a foot on the land that had once been his father's and should now be his. He came to a small, stony path leading up into the pines. Winter rains and summer storms had caused water to erode it and now it was more of a gully than a path.

Abruptly he came in sight of his house. It crouched on a flat area backed by pines. In the half-light it looked what it was – an old abandoned building.

Drac was not a sentimental man. He had never thought of the house as home. If he ever thought of home, and in prison he had always sought to banish such thoughts as signs of weakness, it was a small house in the Forêt des Maures where he had lived with his mother while his father had been in the army. That had been during the World War not 'his' wars in Indo-China and Algeria.

After his mother died, his father had sold up and bought this place and the two of them had lived together. They had hated each other, which was why Drac had joined the army, to get away from home. He had fought in Indo-China and in the Battle of Algiers and the whole thing was nearly over when they bombed the bar in Oran. His buddy had been killed and Drac had taken splinters in the leg. They thought at first he'd have to have it off but they had managed to save it and he'd gone home with a disability pension. It wasn't much, but his father constantly tried to borrow from him to buy liquor. When he refused there were rows.

He walked to the door of the house and put down his suitcase. The place was built of stone, so little on the outside was changed except the growth of trees and bushes. He had been there when the police had padlocked the front door. He had asked them to let him close it up properly but they said there wasn't time. Now the padlock was gone, the door hung on its hinges. The shutters had been stolen and some of the window panes were smashed.

'Home,' he said to the dog.

He tied its lead to the branch of a tree, then opened the suitcase and took out a packet of candles. The night was clear and frosty. He lit one of the candles and pulled open the door. Holding the light above his head he went in. The interior was a ruin. You can't walk away from a house and leave it for twenty years and expect to come back and find it as you left it, he told himself.

The police had asked him what he wanted to do with the furniture, and he'd said leave it where it was. Wasn't there someone, they said, who could look after it for him?

He had thought of the people in La Motte. There was no one there he could ask, no one who would do it for him if he did. His father had not been a popular figure in the village, nor had Drac himself. They were still outsiders after fifteen years. It was that kind of community. He remembered when he had buried his father. There was only the priest and himself at the graveside. To hell with them, he thought, they'd have to put up with him now.

He lit the other candles and placed them round what had once been the kitchen/living-room. The walls were unplastered and the stone was covered in dust and cobwebs.

People had been in the house over the years, perhaps even lived here. Fires had been made in the old black range and food had been cooked on it. Pots, encrusted with something ancient and nameless, lay on the floor; chairs had been broken up and used for fuel. He went upstairs to the bedroom. The bed in which he and Yvette had slept was gone. He remembered buying it at the market in Pierrefeu. It had been a brass bedstead and when he and Yvette had made love it had sounded like a Wurlitzer.

There were things that could not be removed or were not worth removing: the old kitchen sink which had to be filled from the well outside, the black cooking range, the walls, the floors.

He went out to the well. It still worked. He pulled up the bucket and gave the dog some water in one of

34

the old pots. 'Take it, Bizetta.' But the dog, even though it must have been thirsty, stood aloof, growling far down in its throat.

He picked up some dead pine branches, made a fire in the range and cleaned an area on the floor near it. He made a pillow of his jacket and lay down on the floor. He did not find it uncomfortable after what he was used to. What worried him was the silence, for gaols are always filled with noise. But he had a bottle of cognac.

He did not blow out the candles, for he was not used to complete darkness either, and lay staring up at the broken ceiling.

Tomorrow he would start on the house. He would also buy food and blankets. Little by little he would make the place habitable. He might even hire someone in Cogolin to do the initial cleaning. After that he would keep it clean himself. And he would cook for himself and look after himself. If he wanted a woman he would go into Toulon. His life would be austere. Just himself and the dog for company. He would prepare himself.

Flora's flat was at the bottom of one of a row of terraced houses in Camden Town. It was called a 'garden flat' by the estate agents, a basement by anyone else. As Jo went down the steps she saw that a light was on behind the heavy curtains. She rang the bell and waited.

Her body was throbbing in various places and she felt stiff and sore. The reaction was producing a feeling of light-headedness, an edge of hysteria she had never felt before. She wanted to burst out laughing and to cry at the same time. She knew that later, when she took off her clothes, she would find bruises. She supposed she was lucky not to have lost teeth. Lucky? You're beaten up, your house is vandalised . . . that's lucky?

She rang again and banged on the door. She thought

she heard sounds from within. She rattled the letter-box flap and shouted through it: 'Flora, it's me!'

A minute or more passed before the door was opened. Flora was wearing a dressing-gown, her dark hair was ruffled and she did not seem pleased to see Jo.

'I was just getting into the bath,' she said.

'I'm sorry, but something's happened. I've been mugged, burglarised, broken into, grievous bodily harmed . . .'

Flora stepped aside and let her in. There was a bedroom to the right of the passage – the door was closed – ahead were the kitchen and bathroom. Jo went into the living-room on the left.

Its over-all colour scheme was white: white leather sofa and chairs, off-white carpet, pale grey etchings on the wall and heavy black curtains. It was a dramatic room, like Flora herself. There was a vodka bottle on the low smoked-glass coffee table and two glasses; the ashtray was full and the air was thick with the smell of tobacco.

Flora was wearing heavy make-up and her lips were a red slash. The lipstick looked newly applied. She gave Jo a drink, took one herself and said, 'Tell me.'

She was a good listener and did not interrupt. When Jo was finished, she said, 'Jesus! You poor thing!' She put her arms round her and held her tight. It was then the second reaction hit, and Jo felt tears gush down her cheeks. Flora patted her head and stroked her hair as she sometimes had done when she was a child. 'Poor baby!'

'It was horrible.'

'Of course it was. You did exactly what he said?'

'God, yes! I haven't even called the police. Not yet anyway.'

'You say his name was Willi?'

'That's what he said. Tell Mick Willi was here.'

'It's obviously a case of mistaken identity.'

'That's what I said. I told him you've got the wrong

36

people, I'm not the one you want to kill. But he said he was sure. You know, he had that absolute certainty that gave me the horrors.'

'It doesn't make sense.' Flora shook her head. 'Unless . . .'

'What?'

'While you were talking I was thinking, what if Mike has got on to something really valuable, a painting perhaps . . .'

'But—'

'It's a vicious world, antiques, especially when there's big money involved.'

'But why would he break up the house?'

'Maybe he didn't break it up . . . I mean, maybe he didn't come to break it up. Maybe he came to look for something. Say it was something small that Mike had bought on that last trip to Europe. Small and valuable. And someone wanted to steal it. The damage could have been done while he was looking for it.'

'Why would he say tell Mike – Mick – Willi was here? You don't do that if you've come to rob someone. You don't leave messages. No, I had the feeling it was a warning. And what he did to me was a warning too. But what about? And why?'

'It was just an idea.' Flora said.

'I need to use the loo.'

'You know where it is.'

She went to the bathroom. When she came back, Flora was pouring herself another drink.

'I tried to phone you,' Jo said. 'You were engaged.'

'I'd forgotten to put the bedroom phone back on the hook.'

'What do we do now? Or rather, what do I do? I don't want to go back there, not tonight anyway.'

'Of course you don't. You'll stay here. When's Mike coming home?'

'Tomorrow. But you can never tell with Mike. If he goes after something he wants, it could be a couple of days.'

Mr Whoozit had been here, Jo thought. Flora was slightly slurred, there were the two glasses, the cigarettes. And there was no water in the bath. She'd been bonking, as Mike called it. That's why the phone had been taken off the hook. 'I'm sorry if I interrupted anything,' she said.

'Don't be silly, you didn't interrupt anything.'

'Harry wanted to see you.'

'Harry?'

'Harry Evans.'

'Oh, that Harry. He came earlier. Wanted to buy something from me.'

'A present, for some old man.'

'A coffee grinder. The one you were putting on the stall. You remember.'

The phone rang. There were two phones in the flat. One in the bedroom and one here in the living-room. Flora hesitated for a second as though deciding which one she was going to answer. Then she picked up the one beside her.

'Hi ...' she said. Then, 'We were just talking about you ... No ... She's here, that's why you couldn't ...' She held out the phone to Jo. 'It's Mike.'

Jo took the phone. 'Oh Mike! God, am I glad to hear your voice.' She knew its timbre so well, deep, well-modulated.

'I tried to get you at home,' he said.

'I must have been on my way over to Flora's.'

'Is everything all right? You sound ...'

'It is now.'

'What does that mean?'

She told him briefly.

'My God, Joey! What a hell of a thing! Are you sure you're all right?'

'Bruised, and for a while bloody nearly bowed.'

'And he said his name was Willi?'

'Yes. He seemed to know you.'

'Listen, I'm on the motorway. I was just phoning to tell you to wait up for me. The traffic's foul but I should be home in about an hour. Why don't you have a drink with Flora . . .'

'I've had one.'

'Have another.'

'I don't want to go into the house by—'

'I know, I know.' His voice was soft, concerned. Then she heard a sudden rush of noise, as though someone had opened the door of the phone booth. There was a rumble of voices, traffic noise, then Mike's again. 'Someone wants to use the bloody phone. Listen, stay where you are, I'll pick you up there.'

Roger Maillet waited in Pimlico, a block away from Jo's house, until after midnight, then he drove slowly over Chelsea Bridge and found parking outside his apartment on Prince of Wales Drive in Battersea. A wind had come up and was shaking the black trees in the park. He was cold and tired and has not eaten since breakfast and this combination had produced a headache and a depression which settled on him like dust.

He was often like this at the end of a day and it was only the memory of her body that kept him going. Belsen . . . Ravensbruck . . . Dachau . . . these were the words the vision conjured up – not Cannes. Not fat Cannes with its Rue Meynadier loaded with gastronomic delights. But it had been in Cannes that he had identified the body. She had looked like a skeleton.

He let himself into his apartment, locked the door behind him and threw the parka on a chair. The place looked terrible. The curtains in the living-room were still closed from the previous night. There was the debris of a meal on the low, tiled coffee table and the room reeked of cigarette smoke.

He went into the kitchen. Several days' washing up was stacked in the sink. He made himself a cup of *filtre* and stood staring out of the kitchen window as he drank it. He knew what was happening to him and he knew he should pull himself together.

It had started when Marie-Claire left him and went back to Paris.

He had seen it happen to other men in the office when their marriages broke up or their girlfriends said goodbye. The drinking, the un-ironed shirts, the sleazy apartments, the desperate need for company. He had thought it could never happen to him, but it had. He lit a cigarette and saw his reflection in the window: a man of medium height, dark, hair untidy and in need of trimming. His face was drawn and thin and there were lines of exhaustion round his eyes. Christ, he thought, I'm thirty-two years old and I look a hundred.

He showered, got into his pyjamas and a dressing-gown and went into the room they had been keeping for the child that had never come. Now he used it as his work-room. It was small and dark and he switched on the word-processor. The screen lit up green and immediately he felt less alone. That was also something he would have to watch. When a computer became your only friend things were going downhill fast.

He pushed in the discs and brought up text. He stared for a long time at the winking cursor and then began to type:

Sunday: am and pm at Camden Lock Market. Arrived ten-thirty. JT setting up stall. Watched her for an hour. Sister arrived about noon. JT looks so innocent; like a schoolgirl. I remind myself that schoolgirls have been known to commit murder . . .

40

7

Not much more than a mile away, in the bedroom of the house in Pimlico, Jo lay in the big double-bed and felt Mike's weight on top of her. He was finished, spent, and so was she, but she could still feel him inside her and she did not want him to move. His slack weight was half smothering her but that's what she wanted. She wanted to lose herself in him. She tightened her arms, drawing him closer . . .

Making love had not been in her mind as they had entered the house. She had been dreading the moment, but Mike had taken her hand and they had gone inside. The hand contact was the first thing. Her body was so full of tension she'd had to restrain herself from biting it, sinking her teeth into the pad of his flesh below the little finger.

'Christ!' he had said as he switched on the living-room light and saw the damage.

'I'll clear it up. I'll have it back the way it was.'

'Not now.' He'd closed the door. 'Let's leave it to the morning.'

'But—'

'No buts. You've had a hell of a time. It can wait.'

'Oh, Mike.' She turned. 'I'm so bloody glad you're home.'

He kissed her then and she felt as though a reservoir was bursting inside her. She was not even sure how they got to the bedroom but she knew she had been like an animal. Now she was peaceful, quiet. This was reality, everything else was a dream.

But another voice inside her skull told her not to be a fool. It was quite the reverse. This was the dream, reality lay behind the closed door of the living-room, reality was in the street, at the market.

'Are you awake?' she said softly.

'Mmmm . . .' he rolled away from her and lit a cigarette.

'Mike?'

'What?'

When he had arrived at Flora's he had made her go through everything in detail. When she had asked her own questions he had said they would talk when they got home. She did not want to talk about it now, yet she knew she could not put it off.

'What?' he said again.

'What are we going to do?'

'That's what I'm trying to work out.'

'I mean, *we* know he made a mistake. Didn't he?'

'Of course he did!'

'But he knew your name.'

'That's just it. He didn't. He said . . . give me the exact words.'

'Tell Mick Willi was here.'

'Have you ever heard anyone call me Mick?'

'No . . .' She smiled in spite of her fears. 'I'd never have married you. Mick Townsend! Mickey Townsend! Mrs Mickey Townsend!'

'See?'

She put her head on his chest. 'I'd seen him before, you know.'

'Who?'

'Willi.'

'You didn't tell me that! Where?'

'At the market. He had a feather in his hat. A kind of Tyrolean hat.'

Mike got out of bed. In the dim light against the nylon curtains she looked at his big frame. He was putting on weight. He had a belly now. All that starch in hotel dining-rooms. He brushed his heavy dark hair back with his hand in a familiar gesture then tied the belt of his dressing-gown and switched on the bedside light. He lit another cigarette. His face had filled out too, she thought, since they had been married. He was a big man, six foot three, and heavy. When they went out together her head barely reached his shoulder.

'And there was another man. He was taking photographs but I think he was watching me too.'

Mike frowned. 'Tell me about him.' She told him. She could see she wasn't convincing him. It all sounded lame, almost neurotic. 'Probably my imagination,' she said. Then, 'Mike, does any of this make sense?'

'None whatsoever.'

'It's all such a mix-up!'

'Why don't you get some sleep,' he said. 'You must be exhausted.'

'My brain's running like a fast forward video.'

'Here, take a pill.' He gave her one from a drawer by the bed.

'What about you? I want you with me.'

'Of course.' He got back into bed and put an arm around her and she fell asleep almost instantly. Sometime during the night she woke, feeling blurry from the pill. She was alone. She felt an instant of terror. Then she saw that his pillows were dented and remembered he was home – and that's all that mattered. In a moment she was sinking back into sleep.

The dog stood by its pot of water and watched Drac come up the track to the house. Drac had walked the

43

three kilometres into La Motte to buy bread, meat and coffee. No one had recognised him and he had recognised no one. He could not even remember the interiors of the shops. Everything was new to his eyes.

He carried a plastic bag in each hand. In one was food, in the other a few pieces of equipment for the kitchen. The rest he would pick up at the Codec in Cogolin later. He would also have to buy himself a car. In the meantime he had to take care of himself and the dog.

He stoked up the fire in the range and put on water to heat for coffee, then he went outside.

'You like meat?' he said, cutting up the beef he had bought. He threw a piece to the dog. It landed in the dirt at its feet. It looked at Drac then at the meat and in one savage grab took it and swallowed it.

'Good? Here's another.'

Each time he threw a piece he moved a little nearer to the dog. It ate the meat but growled at him, straining at the leash.

'You're frightened,' Drac said. 'That's why you want to bite me. But if I let you go you'd run away.'

He went inside, fetched his coffee and broke up the bread, dunking it in the hot liquid. It tasted good. Better than the prison bread.

'Oh, yes,' he said to the dog. 'Much better.' He threw it the last of the meat and watched it wolf it down. 'No gypsy ever gave you raw beef.'

The dog was looking away from him, growling deep in its throat. A man was coming up the track. From fifty metres he was recognisable to Drac as a cop. He leaned against the wall of the house and waited. He had been expecting this.

The policeman reached the level ground and stopped. The dog kept up its low growling. Drac was glad to see that some kind of territorial association had already taken

44

place in its mind, for it seemed to dislike the cop more than it disliked him.

'Is that your dog?' the cop said.

'Yes.'

'You want to take care. It looks vicious to me.'

'I'm going to get a chain. He guards the house.'

'It's your house?'

'Yes.'

'You Drac? Marcel Henri Drac?'

'That's right. And this is my house, what's left of it.'

The cop shrugged. 'That's what happens when you leave your property for twenty years. You expect everything to be the same?'

'No.'

'Good. Because nothing is going to be the same.' He took his handkerchief, dusted the surface of an old log and sat down on it. He was short and square and his hair was cut *en brosse*. His eyes were widely spaced. Drac thought he had the face of a peasant, but the kind of peasant who knows his stuff. There had been men like him in the army: tough sods who never took any shit from anyone, not even the officers.

Drac lowered his head. 'I know,' he said.

'I don't want people like you on my beat, Drac. I like things calm and nice. Understand?' His eyes were cold. 'Where did you steal the dog?'

'I swear—'

'They don't let you have pets inside. You got out yesterday. Where did you steal it?'

Drac explained but the cop waved him into silence.

'All right, I'll check. I'm going to check everything you say and do. Every time you go for a piss, I'm going to check. Understand?'

'Yes.'

The cop rose and walked away, then turned. 'You

45

remember what I said. And remember who said it. My name is Dubois.'

Drac and the dog watched Dubois make his way down the track and disappear into the pines. After a few moments they heard a car start and then the engine noise faded away as it went down towards the main road.

'It's good to know the enemy,' Drac said to the dog.

Mike woke Jo at eleven. She came back to life slowly, woozy from the pill. He was standing by the bed with a mug of black coffee. It was the smell more than anything else that woke her. She took it gratefully and then put out a hand to take his.

'I dreamt you weren't here. But you are.'

He was dressed in honey-coloured corduroy slacks, a double-breasted dark blue blazer, pink shirt and paisley silk square knotted at the throat. He looked every inch the ex-army officer.

'That was some pill,' she said. 'It knocked me flat.'

'It was one of mine. When you're feeling okay we must talk.'

She showered and then went back to the living-room. It was tidy and clean and there was no evidence it had been vandalised.

'I was going to do it,' she said.

'You've had enough. That's what we have to talk about.'

He was half hidden by the curtain, looking out at the street. Rain was dripping down the window panes. She knew he was watching for the watcher and she shivered in spite of the warmth of the heating. But at the same time she felt angry.

'You've got to get away,' he said.

'Why? This is our house! To hell with it! Anyway you're here now.' Mike was big and even though he was running to, well, fat, he still looked powerful and dangerous. If she was Willi she wouldn't fancy mixing it with Mike.

46

He turned from the window. 'Did you lock the double locks?'

'When?'

'Yesterday. When you went to the market.'

She had been half expecting the question. 'No.'

'Christ, Joey, how often—'

'I know, I know.'

'What's the point of having expensive locks fitted if you don't use them?'

He had an uncanny ability to wrong-foot her. 'I'm sorry. Anyway, where would we go?'

'Not we. You.'

'What are you going to do?'

'Cause a diversion.'

'A diversion from *what*? Mike, we're the wrong people, remember? You said so yourself. He'll know by now. Anyway, now that you're back we can go to the police.'

'He warned you about that.'

'We can't just pretend nothing happened.'

He rubbed his right cheek in a gesture she knew well: he did it before he was going to lie to her or tell her something he knew she would not like. As an actress she had picked up the trick herself and used it several times.

'There is something else, Joey.'

She felt as though a cold hand had squeezed her stomach.

'What?' Her voice was not much more than a whisper.

'I found something on my last trip to Vienna. It could be worth a bloody fortune.'

'Flora said so!'

'Flora said what?'

'That you'd probably found something small but valuable. And that the antiques trade played rough when big money was involved. Why didn't you tell me?'

'I didn't want to worry you.'

'What is it?'

He went to a weeping ficus growing in a terracotta pot near the window, lifted the tree from the pot and felt underneath. He brought out a plastic bag and put it gently on the table. He opened it and she found herself looking at a little figurine. It was some sort of animal and seemed to be made of plaster of Paris.

'What is it' she repeated.

'It's a vicuña. A kind of llama.' He stood it on the table. It was about three inches high. Its long graceful neck was turned so that it looked at them as if in mild surprise.

'It's beautiful,' she said.

'Pre-Colombian. From Peru.'

'How much do . . . ? Is it valuable?'

'It's worth maybe half a million.'

'What!'

'That's a guess. But a pretty good one.'

'My God!' She put out a hand to touch it. 'Is it some sort of ceramic?'

'That's just a covering.' He touched the dusty, clay-coloured figure. 'Underneath that is pure gold.'

She let out her breath. 'No wonder . . . And he . . . the man . . . you got it from?'

'He's a dealer. Moves between South America and Europe. This was bought from a . . . a syndicate in Lima.'

'But that's illegal, isn't it? Trading in pre-Colombian art?'

He smiled and went to the window again. 'Very illegal.'

'So?'

'So the man who bought this in Lima originally was robbed by a taxi driver on the way to the airport. Apparently it happens quite often. You buy something like this and there's no way you can go to the police if it's stolen. And mainly it's stolen back by the people who sold it to you in the first place. Some pieces are sold over and over again.

'How did this piece get out then?'

'The thing is, the taxi driver was robbed too. By someone else, who did manage to get it out.'

'And you bought it from him?'

'Not exactly.'

He rubbed his cheek again.

She said, 'You stole it.'

'I expropriated it. You can't steal something that isn't owned.'

'And this man you "expropriated" it from, he's the one who . . .'

'Willi.'

She sat down. 'And it was there all the time?' She pointed to the ficus.

'I didn't want to worry you. Anyway, I didn't think he'd come to London. He's wanted here by the police. For God's sake, Joey, I'd never have kept it in the house if I'd thought . . .'

'But what are we going to do? He's not just going to forget about it. Why don't we go to the police and tell them who he is?'

'You're not thinking straight. What are we going to tell them? That a man you've never seen before beat you up and wrecked the flat? And you *think* he's someone from Vienna who maybe was mixed up in some illegal antiquities deal in Peru. See?'

'But you know him. You could convince them and then they'd pick him up and . . .'

'Pick him up where? You don't think he came in under his own name, do you? It could take them weeks to trace him. By that time he'd be back in Vienna or South America or Timbuktu and meanwhile I've got mixed up in this and have to explain what the hell I'm doing with a valuable piece of Inca art which I acquired . . . how?

49

Receipt please, Mr Townsend. And then someone tips off the Peruvian Embassy and the shit hits the fan.'

'So you're going to keep it.'

'That's right.'

'And Willi?'

'I can deal with Willi, but not if you're around.'

'What does that mean? What do you mean "deal" with him?'

'Frighten him.'

'Mike, you're not Batman. This isn't TV.'

'I realise that. Listen Jo, I know this sort of person. I do business with them. He won't try anything on with me. But he'll go after me through you. And I can't be with you every minute of the day. Anyway, I've got to go to Wales tomorrow. I told you. There's an antiques fair at Cardiff.'

'You don't *have* to go. You can give this one a miss.'

'No I can't. When would I stop "giving things a miss"?'

'I could stay with Flora.'

'For ever? Anyway she's not there. She called while you were asleep to find out how you were. She's gone away with you know who for a few days.'

'Mr Whoozit?'

'That's right.' He rubbed his face again. 'Listen Joey, this is the first really big thing that's come my way. I know someone in Italy who'd pay me half a million, maybe more, for this, and no questions asked. Think what it would mean to us! We could sell this place and—'

'I don't want to sell this place!'

'You've always said it was too small for a kid.'

She paused. 'A child?'

'Maybe two, three.'

'But you never . . .'

'I always said we'd need money first. Kids can cost a fortune. Specially schooling.'

'You're jumping ahead a bit.' She felt a sudden surge of excitement.

'It's true. Just think about it. We could get a place in the country if you wanted to. Something really good.'

'But what about Willi? He's not just going to say goodbye vicuña.'

'That'll be the Italian's problem. It's the figurine Willi wants, not me.'

'You mean "it's just business"?'

'Precisely. And it's not even unusual. I mean, are you sure that all the things you've bought for the stall were kosher? In the antiques business we'd all go bust if we had to verify everything.'

That was true, she thought. Some things just fell off the backs of lorries. You sort of knew that, yet you didn't ask questions. If Mike was right and this piece had been owned by a gang in Lima and they sold it over and over and robbed each buyer, then why not?

She said, 'I'll come with you to Wales.'

He shook his head. 'I told you. The buyer lives in Italy.'

'So how are we—' She stopped short, then said, 'Mike, it isn't *we*, is it? It's *me*!'

'I want you to take it to France. I'll join you there.'

'You want me to . . . ? Oh, no!'

Suddenly he was impatient. 'For Christ's sake Jo. I need your help. I don't often ask.'

'But—'

'But me no buts, as the man said. I want you to take it to La Motte. To your house.'

'She felt a sudden choking sensation as though all the muscles in her throat were tightening. Then she said, 'I'm not going there, Mike. I'm never going there.'

Jean-Claude Dubois spent the better part of the morning on the Route du Canadel – not on police business. There was an enclave of holiday homes a kilometre

51

beyond Drac's house, built in the past twenty years by a speculative developer from Lyons. Their architecture was Spanish-Californian: tiled roofs and wrought iron. Each had a swimming pool and each was hidden behind its own wall.

Dubois opened the big steel gates of the first house and drove up to the front where the name SYLT was picked out on the wall in sea shells. He opened an attaché case. The interior was divided into sections, each with a name and a bunch of keys. He took out a bunch marked Lindemann and unlocked the house. He stood in the living-room and sniffed. There was no smell of damp, but the house was cold.

The floor was of Provençal tiles and the throw-rugs had been rolled up against the wall. He flicked on a fan heater and then made his tour of the house. He checked the thermostat on the central heating, felt the just-warm radiators, checked the oil level in the tank at the back. It was getting low and he would have to re-order. He checked the gutterings and the pipes, checked that the water in the loos contained anti-freeze, checked the window catches. Then he locked up the house leaving the fan heater running low. The place could do with a circulation of air so that mould would not form. He checked the swimming pool, he checked the gas barbecue. He was satisfied. He drove to the next house.

He inspected each house in turn, switching on heaters where he thought it was necessary. By lunchtime he had checked all eight houses. In a few days he would come back and check again. He did this once a week at least, sometimes twice if the weather was bad, from October to April until the owners came south.

He drove back along the road, past the turn-off to Drac's house, past the Englishman's house – they still called it that even though he had been dead for years. He came to the main road and turned towards Cogolin.

It was nearly twelve o'clock. He stopped at a *boulangerie*, bought two baguettes and drove to his apartment in Grimaud. It was a large apartment and had a view of the sea and his colleagues who had never been inside would have been surprised at the richness of its interior.

He was met at the door by his wife, Josephine. Where Dubois was short and square, Josephine was large and soft. She was some years older than her husband and was looking a bit frayed at the edges. But she was still something to look at.

She was wearing a white jump-suit and red high-heeled pumps. Gold chains hung from her neck and gold bangles from her wrists. Her hair was orange-blonde and her make-up hectic. She was taller than Dubois and he liked to think of her as Juno-esque because he had heard the word somewhere. Some of his colleagues, less kind, said she had the buttocks of a Percheron. They were clearly delineated through the thin material and her mini-pants cut into her giving her silhouette a corrugated look.

Josephine had been on the game in Nice for many years when Dubois was on foot patrol. He had arrested her several times when the pressure was on and the moral indignation of the city fathers was brought out and dusted.

She had given him the odd present for all the times he hadn't arrested her and they had grown to like each other. Then had come an occasion when Josephine had felt age and mortality creeping up on her.

'Oh, not again, *chéri*,' she said. 'You and I must come to some agreement.'

She had visited his apartment that night. It was a typical bachelor pad, cold and functional. Just seeing her in it had changed Dubois' view of life. She gave it colour, drama, interest. They had gone to bed and afterwards she had looked at him and said with some surprise, 'I enjoyed that.'

It had been the beginning for them. The tart and

the cop was an old relationship, but this blossomed. After a few months, when Dubois was transferred to Cogolin, they married. Dubois himself came from a hill farm in the Ardèche and had inherited the peasant's cunning. She added to that the guile of the streets. Soon they were thriving.

To look at she was a dumb and dizzy middle-aged blonde. It was a part she played to perfection. She had bought herself a chihuahua called Toutou which nested on her great rounded bosom.

As she greeted Dubois at the door she said to the dog, which wore a perpetually vexed expression, 'Here's papa, *chéri*. Say hello to papa.'

Toutou gave papa a look of intense dislike but Dubois was impervious to the dog's moods. He tolerated it as one might tolerate a piece of live junk jewellery.

They made a good lunch of *potage*, Westphalian ham (a present from the Lindemanns of Hamburg), a bottle of Grösl lager (a present from the Van der Meulens of Amsterdam) and finished off with a cognac (the Jonssons of Gothenburg) and a couple of chocolate truffles (Madame Rival of Geneva).

'Did papa see him?' she asked her husband through Toutou.

Dubos nodded. 'He's got a dog. Savage-looking brute.'

'They won't like that,' she said. 'I mean if it starts digging up their gardens.'

'Never mind the gardens. What about old Madame Rival's cat? And the Lindemanns have a new poodle. I'm telling you, one mouthful, that's all it'd be for that brute of Drac's.'

'Cover your ears!' she said to Toutou and pulled him into her cleavage.

Dubois lit a half corona (the Greshoffs from The Hague) and sat smoking quietly. Then he said, 'Just our luck. Just when things are going well.'

'You think he'll . . . ?'

'I don't know what he'll do. Just being there's enough. I want peace and quiet on my patch, otherwise why is anyone going to pay me? All right, I see to their houses in the winter, but any fool can do that. What they want from me is protection, security. And for that they pay well for seven months a year. And now here comes a murderer and sits down in the middle of them. What can Dubois do about it? That's what I would be asking if I were the Jonssons with grandchildren coming down July and August.'

'He'll make a mistake,' Josephine said.

'Sure. I told him that. I said every time you go for a piss I'll be checking on you.'

'The dog's easy,' she said. 'We can deal with that.'

'Maybe.' He rose. 'I must get back to the station. One good thing: he gives me a reason for going up there. The Chief's been a bit nosey lately.'

'What would you like tonight, *chéri*?'

'Steak.'

That's what he wanted every night, she thought. Sometimes oysters with it. And only the best. Well, why not? They could afford it.

8

Portsmouth in the rain, ten-thirty p.m.

Jo had never liked Portsmouth. She had not visited it since her grandmother had died, which was so long ago that she did not know the new motorways into the city, so she took a route that ran endlessly through dreary streets until she finally saw a sign saying CHANNEL FERRIES and BRITANNIA LINE. She had been afraid she might miss the ferry and this had added to the tension that lay in her stomach like some great knotted fist.

She had been feeling sick with apprehension all the way from London. In her time she had smuggled the odd bottle of cognac through customs and, as a young teenager, had, on a dare, shoplifted sweets in Woolworths. This was the extent of her criminal experience.

The figurine hung in front of her as she drove, suspended on a piece of elastic that was tied to the rear-view mirror. 'They'll never give it a glance,' Mike had said.

She had to remind herself each time the tension gripped her, of something else he had said. 'How many times have you been to France? Twenty? Thirty? Have you *ever* known the French customs to stop you?'

She had to admit she had never been stopped, nor seen any other British car searched either.

She turned into the ferry terminal's car park. The rain was lashing down and there was hardly a human being to be seen under the orange lights.

She was waved to a place in the queue for the

Cherbourg ferry by a man in a glistening slicker. Everyone else seemed to be huddled in the ticket office. There were about twenty cars making for Cherbourg, and the same number queuing for Le Havre.

They began to load immediately. As she drove the VW bus towards passport control, she felt again a tightening of tension. She pulled up at the window, but all she saw was a hand groping for her passport. In a second it had been returned to her and she was moving towards the ship's cavernous maw.

The *Duke of Hampshire* was an old ferry and everything about her looked old, from the rust-streaked hull to the worn carpets. There was a smell of vomit and disinfectant in the bar, which did not seem to bother a group of truck drivers who were sitting in a corner drinking whisky with beer chasers.

She wandered about the ship, clutching her shoulder bag. She had taken the figurine off its elastic and placed it between two sanitary napkins. She felt as though she was carrying a live grenade.

The ship sailed before midnight, slipping out past half a dozen Royal Naval frigates and the fun-fair at Southsea, whose coloured lights were hazy and sad in the rain.

This was usually an experience she enjoyed. She had first crossed to France with her grandmother, then on school trips and then with boyfriends.

And then she had crossed with Mike. If he had been there now, they would have been up on deck having a drink of malt whisky from his flask and watching the lights disappear, because, as he always said, the farther they were from England the nearer they were to France – and that was something to celebrate.

When she could no longer see the lights she went to her cabin and lay on the bunk. The taste of adventure was not there this time: that expectancy of landing in France, that first smell of black tobacco and urine and cooking, of not knowing what was just around the corner – it wasn't there at all. Instead, there was fear.

She realised now that it was not so much the fear of what she was carrying with her – she knew that Mike was right about that – it was the fear of where she was going. That was what had caused their major argument.

She had refused point blank to go to the house but he had simply not accepted it. She had used all the old arguments which she had so often used on herself and Flora but without going into detail, because even now she could not face the details. He had simply absorbed them like a sponge.

They had talked for hours until finally he had worn her down. She had grown tired, confused.

'You can't run away forever,' he had said.

She had suggested hotels they had been to before but he had dismissed them all.

'What if you can't get a room? What if the car breaks down? I won't be at the end of a phone. No, it's got to be the house. Then I'll know exactly where you are. I'll call you there not tomorrow night but the next and tell you when I'm arriving . . . . Listen Joey, it's only for a few days. I'll go down to Cardiff and shake off Willi. He'll be watching for me now, not you. Then back up to the Channel coast. I won't even return to London. And I'll grab the first ferry I can. I promise.'

'And then?'

'And then we'll take the corniche to Italy and get rid of this thing and have the holiday of our lives.'

The mention of Willi's name had brought back the terror she had felt when he had hit her. She couldn't cope with that again. Anything would be better than that. Even the house in France. So finally she had agreed.

She switched off the light and lay on the bunk in the darkness, listening to the thump-thump-thump of the propellers and the creaking and groaning of the bulkheads. And she thought: I don't want to be here.

She slept badly, her mind filled with uneasy thoughts that lay just out of reach and turned to dreams. She was glad when morning came and she was able to go up on deck and watch the hills behind Cherbourg materialise out of the heavy overcast. It was raining here too.

She was almost the first to reach the car deck and she tied the figurine on to the stem of the rear-view mirror once again, thinking, as she did so, how much she normally hated cars with dingly-danglies hanging in front of the drivers.

As she waited, she watched the other drivers come to their cars. Some of the huge trucks had already started up their diesels. A man three rows away from her caught her eye. His back was towards but there was something about the shape of his head . . . She looked more closely, but he opened the door of his silver-grey Saab, got in and was immediately obscured by other cars.

She frowned. There had just been something about him . . . God, if she went on this way *everyone* would begin to look familiar and full of menace.

No one except Mike knew she was here. She had always like the anonymity of travelling in France, the knowledge that no one knew where she was or what she was doing, and she was grateful for it now.

The ship's bow doors opened and the loading ramp came down. Soon the vehicles were moving. She was concentrating: *drive on the right . . . drive on the right . . .*

The rain was as hard as it had been in Portsmouth and the quays were deserted. She followed the stream of traffic to passport and customs control. Again her stomach was gripped by icy fear, yet her face and brow felt flushed. She tried to dispel all thoughts of what she was doing. If you *look* guilty, you *are* guilty, she thought.

But like their British counterparts the French officials preferred to be inside on days like this. An arm came out of the passport control window. She held out her passport but the arm waved her through in an irritated fashion as though she was holding up the line of cars.

She followed a truck as it ground its way through Cherbourg and into the hills behind the town, and then she hit the dual carriageway and she was free and running. She shoved a cassette of Dave Brubeck into the stereo. But the melody was 'Lonesome Road' and it filled her with such sadness that she switched to a tape of the Quintet of the Hot Club of France.

She shot down the Cotentin Peninsula, then stopped in Domfront and had coffee and brioche at the Hôtel de la Poste. She took a road map in with her and studied it. She should be heading in the direction of Paris to pick up the autoroute to Marseilles, but she suddenly realised that the longer she was on the road, the less time she would have to spend in the house. Mike wasn't due to call her until the following night. If he wanted her to do this for him, then she'd do it in style. It was his money.

She made a rough plan: she would lunch somewhere on the Loire then, to elongate the journey still further, she would take the autoroute via Toulouse. That way she might only reach the house after Mike had arrived. She might not even have to spend a minute there, let alone hours or days.

She had lunch in Saumur, sitting in a window over-looking the Loire and watching two boys fishing under the bridge. Then she made for the autoroute south of Tours. By mid-afternoon her shoulders and neck were aching and when she saw the sign for Saintes she decided to spend the night there.

It was five o'clock, hysteria time in France. On pre-vious trips she had passed through many small French towns during the calm afternoons, only to be caught in the five o'clock frenzy when they suddenly filled with cars, students, housewives, tourists, all rushing about the streets, choking the cafés and shops as though everything was instantly going to close. Now she was glad to see them, for she was sick of her own company.

She booked into the Lion d'Or, had a quick shower and changed. She decided to look over the town and pick out a restaurant for later.

As she went down the front steps of the hotel she saw a silver-grey Saab nose its way gently into the hotel's garage.

'Take it', Drac said to the dog. 'Go on, take it.'

They were outside the house in the late afternoon sunshine. Drac was crouched down a yard or more beyond the dog's reach. In front of him was a marrow bone with meat still on it. He had a piece of bamboo in his hand and pushed the bone a few inches closer to the dog.

At his left side was the chain he had bought that morning. He wanted to replace the lead with the chain, but the dog had sensed that something was going on. It was not just a matter of the bone. Its tail was down, the black hair on its neck was raised, its big square head was facing slightly away from Drac but the eyes never left him. Its mouth was half open and Drac saw that the canines were stained brown.

This dog was really something, he thought. It trusted no one. 'You're like me,' he said, as he inched nearer.

When he was a boy living in the middle of the cork oaks of the Forêt des Maures, he had picked up a great deal of lore concerning savage dogs. Every lonely house kept one on a long running wire. The main thing was always to keep talking. Silence rattled a dog when it was already suspicious.

'Yes,' he said softly. 'We're two of a pair.'

He began to hum an old tune that had been popular in the early 1960s. He hummed and sang in a soft, monotonous voice.

61

He had achieved a great deal during the day. He had walked into Cogolin in time for the banks to open, had checked his account and found it as he expected. If he was careful he had enough to last for a long time. Then he had bought a second-hand Renault, had driven to a *supermarche* near Port Grimaud and filled the back of the car with the things he would need to start him off. He had driven back to the house and had started work on the main living-room. At the end of two hours it was looking a different place. But he knew it was only a beginning.

Still humming, he pushed the bone towards the dog so that it was almost touching its forepaws. It growled, a low grating sound. 'You'll enjoy it,' Drac said. 'It's good. It's got meat and it's got marrow. You can get your tongue in the end.'

He raised himself on to the balls of his feet. 'Don't be afraid. No one's going to hurt you. Take the bone.'

He lifted the bamboo and put it gently on the dog's back. It swung round and snapped at it.

'I won't hurt you.' He began to rub up and down the dog's backbone.

The dog endured, growling all the time. The bone was in front of it, the smell all but overwhelming. The feeling of the bamboo rubbing along its spine was pleasurable. It was confused.

Slowly Drac worked the bamboo up the dog's back and slipped it under the studded collar. Then, with a sudden jerk he was on his feet and pulling on the bamboo so that it twisted the collar, choking the dog. Drac managed to get his hand on to the collar.

He held it with one hand, feeling the dog's strength as it fought him. 'Easy. Easy. Take it easy.' With his other hand he fixed the chain to the collar and then, dragging the dog with him, managed to fasten the other end to the tree. He slipped off the lead and leapt to one side. The dog sprang at him but the chain jerked it flat on its back.

He gave the dog the bone and went down to his car. He had brought it a little way up from the road and parked it beneath a pine tree. It wasn't the ideal place but at least it couldn't be seen from the road. He started it, bumped down the track, and then took the road to La Motte. It was time to show himself, time to listen.

9

'This is the Arch of Germanicus.' a voice said at Jo's side.

She swung around. It was dusk and she had been standing on the right bank of the Charente looking over the river to the town, thinking how attractive it was and wondering why no one had ever mentioned it to her before.

She now found herself facing the man who had been driving the Saab. He was dressed in a dark grey corduroy suit and white polo neck sweater. His hair was untidy and blowing slightly in the light breeze. His hand was still stretched out, pointing to the great Roman arch.

'God, you gave me a fright!' she said.

'I apologise.'

They were alone on this side of the river and lights were going on in the town.

She moved past him but he said, 'Wouldn't you like to hear about the Roman remains?'

'No, thank you.'

'This place used to be called Mediolanium.'

'Really?' She increased her pace, making for the bridge that led back to Saintes' main street.

'Yes, really.' Keeping pace with her, he held up a little booklet. 'It says so in here.'

'Would you please leave me alone!'

'I saw you on the ferry.' He had a marked accent but spoke English effortlessly. They were on the bridge. The busy main street, filled with lights and cars and people,

64

was only a hundred metres away. She breathed more easily and slowed her pace.

'Why do you not wish me to talk to you?' he said. 'We are far from home. We should stick together.' He smiled. It changed the whole structure of his face for it stretched up to his eyes and almost closed them. It was a smile of infinite enjoyment and she felt herself wanting to smile in sympathy.

'Look.' He held out his hands then pulled up his sleeves. 'See? Nothing.'

She had moved on but he caught up with her and said, 'I would like to buy you a drink.'

'I'm sorry, but . . .'

'We have shared a common experience. We have travelled on the *Duke of Hampshire*. We are bound together.'

This time she could not help sharing his smile.

'That's better,' he said.

'I'm married,' she said, and winced at the gaucherie.

'Yes. I know.'

'How?' She was instantly alarmed.

'You're wearing a wedding ring. But in France having a drink together is not adultery.'

She thought for a moment, then shrugged. 'You're right. Okay, let's have a drink.'

They went to the nearest café. She had a gin and tonic and he a *pression*.

'My name is Roger.' He gave it the French pronunciation.

'Mine's Joanna. Jo.'

'I like Joanna.'

'You live in France?'

'No. I work for AFP in London.'

'AFP?'

'I'm sorry. I forget that not everyone knows about us. Agence France Presse. I'm going to Cannes to do an interview. And you? What do you do?'

'An actress. Or I would be if someone would give me the parts.'

'And when they don't?'

'We have a house in Pimlico. I look after that. Do a little bit of trading.'

'Trading?'

'Market trading. In what you'd call a flea market.'

'And what do you trade?'

'Junk mainly. It's supposed to be Victorian kitchenware but I can't always find enough.'

They had a second drink. It was dark now and the café had emptied. They were almost the only two customers left.

'I'm going to ask you a great favour, Joanna,' he said.

She was instantly suspicious but he smiled again and raised a hand. 'Nothing indiscreet I assure you. Look, it is now seven-thirty. We both have to eat. Why not eat together? We will then enjoy our meals and pass the evening pleasantly. Otherwise I must go back to the hotel and fetch a book or magazine and sit in some place where the lighting is not good for reading and strain my eyes and become unaware of my food. No true Frenchman can do that.'

'You don't sound like a true Frenchman,' she said. 'Your sense of humour isn't French, or anyway, it's not like any Frenchman I've known.'

'I have a strange and romantic past,' he said. 'Dine with me and I shall tell you about it.'

She had been picked up. There was no question about it. It hadn't happened for a long time and was flattering. Now that she'd had a drink with him she had lost her sense of apprehension. What was more natural than two people, who were travelling the same route, spending a civilised evening together?

'All right. I'd like to.'

'Excellent. I have already booked a table for myself

at the Belle Epoque. But there are always two chairs. Is that not so? It is just up the street.'

The Belle Epoque was a serious French eating-house. The seats were upholstered in red velvet, the wood was black, there were several mirrors which reflected the chandeliers.

Jo momentarily regretted having accepted his invitation as she wondered whether he was going to order an elaborate meal and expensive wine. But he said, 'I like simple food, do you?'

She had been looking down the menu's selection of dishes with heavy sauces, and said with relief, 'I prefer it.'

'We're not too far from Royan. The oysters from there are excellent. You like fish?'

'Love it.'

'Grilled sole off the bone?'

After they had settled for that and a bottle of Sancerre, she said, 'You promised me a strange and romantic story.'

'Do you smoke?' he said.

'I gave it up.'

'Character with beauty. That's rare.'

She felt a sense of pleasure. It was the sort of compliment she knew was simply tossed into the conversation as a gambit, but no one had said anything like it for a long time and she realised she had missed the flattery.

He lit a Gitane and said, 'I hope I didn't raise your expectations. But you're right. I'm not a true Frenchman. Half and half. My father was the export director of the Cognac Association in New York. It was his job to promote cognac in every state and every town and to see that it was in every bar.

'He met my mother there. She worked for the advertising agency the association used. I was born. Educated partly in America, partly in France, took a degree at the

Sorbonne. Went into radio journalism, after that *Le Figaro*, now AFP. There you are.' With his hands he made a kind of book-shaped oblong in the air. 'My Life by Roger Maillet.'

'No girls?' she said.

'Of course.'

'And a wife?'

'A wife too. Marie-Claire. Until a few months ago. But . . .' He looked down at the table, ' . . . it's over.' She waited. 'She did not like London. She had no friends there and I was working strange hours. Often away for days at a time. It is one of the hazards of the job.'

'I'm sorry.'

He raised his shoulders in a true Gallic gesture. 'It was inevitable. She wanted children but no children came. In the beginning she blamed me but then we found it was not me but her.' He mashed out the cigarette.

The oysters came on beds of ice and seaweed. There was brown bread and butter, a slice of lemon, and onion vinegar.

She found that she was starving. The oysters were fat and cold. 'Now,' he said as the shells were taken away. 'Your turn. My Life by Joanna . . .' he raised his eyebrows.

'Townsend.'

'What a very English name.'

'What do you want to know?'

'Everything! The way I would write it. "Joanna Townsend bracket age unbracket . . ."'

'Twenty-seven.'

'Joanna Townsend (27) actress and sometime market trader of Pimlico, London, was born . . .'

'Born in a *clinique* in St Tropez.'

'Amazing. Go on.'

'My father and mother lived in a converted farmhouse back of the coast. He was a playwright. Rollo Fleming. Does the name mean anything to you?'

'No.'

'He wrote Agatha Christie-type mysteries but they haven't been put on for years. Anyway, when I was tiny my mother died. They had been swimming off Pampelonne Beach and she drowned. A few years later my father died. So my sister and I came back to England and were looked after by my grandmother.'

'And the house? Did you sell it?'

'No. At that time it was difficult to get a good price because . . . well, it just was, and my grandmother thought we might as well keep it. It wasn't costing much. Then when we grew up we could sell it if we wanted to.'

'And you have used it as a holiday home?'

'Flora has. I . . . I don't go down very often.'

'You're going there now?'

'The couple from the village who looked after it for us grew too old. The husband died last year and his wife moved to be near her married son in Clermont-Ferrand.'

She heard the lies coming out of her mouth as though spoken by someone else. Not complete lies, partial lies. But she needed to be careful.

They ate their sole and finished their wine and had coffee, then she said, 'Thank you, it's been a lovely evening.' He paid the bill and they went out into the cold and windy night.

The hotel was only a block away. As they were going up the stairs from the pavement he stopped and said, 'And so we go to our chaste couches.'

There was a question mark in his tone and she said, 'That's right.'

He took her hand and raised it to his lips. 'I think I will go for a walk. But first, will you have lunch with me tomorrow?'

'Lunch?'

'We are both travelling the same road. It is a long dreary stretch to Toulouse. It will give me something to

69

look forward to. Then you will go about your business and I mine.'

She smiled. 'That would be nice.'

'Is it time?' Flora said.

'Just about.'

She was sitting astride him, hands on his chest, gently rising and falling. The heat in the bedroom was turned up and as she looked down she could see the sweat on her own naked body. She stopped and lifted a glass of vodka and orange. 'Want some more?'

'I'm driving,' Mike said. 'We don't want something to go wrong for a stupid thing like a drink too many.'

She drank half the glass in one long pull and resumed the gentle rising and falling.

'I could go on like this forever,' she said.

He took her in his arms and twisted her so that she lay on her side next to him. 'You never get enough, do you?' he said.

'Not with you. Oh God, Mike, sometimes I want to . . . I don't know . . . suck your blood . . . ! Eat you!'

'For Christ's sake, don't bite me. Remember Jo.'

'Sweetie, it doesn't matter about Jo any more. It doesn't matter what she sees. We're together now. No more hotel rooms, no more excuses . . . That's how it is, isn't it?'

'Of course.'

'What's the matter?'

'Nothing's the matter.'

'You sound . . . I don't know . . .'

'I'm edgy. Aren't you?'

'Not when I'm with you. Not like this. Not when I'm concentrating on what we're doing to each other. You want a ciggy?'

She took another mouthful of her drink then lit two cigarettes and gave him one. 'I nearly did that the other night.'

'What?'

'When you came in for Jo. Lit two cigarettes and gave you one. It's a very intimate gesture, you know.'

'I'm glad you didn't, it would have screwed up everything.'

She lay back, smoking, using her other hand on him.

'It's going to be marvellous! No more Mr Whoozit. Mike, do you really, honest to God, think it's going to work?'

'Why not? She's got it. She takes it to the house. Bob's your uncle.'

'What about Willi?'

'What about him?'

'I mean . . . I don't really trust him . . .'

'Of course you don't. Nor do I. That's why we're doing it this way.'

'Yes, I know. Trust isn't quite the word. I mean I wouldn't be surprised if he, you know, did something funny.'

'What? Monologues, things like that?'

'Don't be daft. You know what I mean.'

'Fuck Willi!'

'You fuck him, sweetie; I'll fuck you.'

He looked at his watch again.

'How long have we got?'

'Fifteen minutes.'

'Oh, that's lots of time.' She stubbed out her cigarette and turned to him. 'I'll tell you one thing,' she said, her hand moving up and down his body, 'I've never wanted anyone as much as I want you.'

'That's nice.'

'Is that all you can say?'

'Christ! What do you want me to say? I want you too. I've said it a dozen times!'

'It's nice to hear.' After a moment she said, 'Willi's a problem though.'

71

'Nothing's going to happen.'

'How do you know? He wasn't supposed to—'

'All right, he went too far. Bloody fool. He was supposed to scare her, okay? That was his way of going about it. Anyway, I talked to him afterwards. I told him I'd break his arm if he wasn't careful.'

'What did he say?'

'Who cares what he said? He's just a bloody stupid bastard.'

She climbed on top of him again. 'Ride a cock horse . . . to Banbury Cross . . .'

Later they got dressed in the dark and Mike said, 'You said Harry was coming to look after the place.'

'That's right. He's going to live here.'

'Well, don't switch on any lights. Just switch off the heating. We'll go out the back way.'

'Why? Is Willi here?'

'Of course he's here.'

'But I thought—'

'Look, I told him I'd be here. Which means he's supposed to think I'll be in Pimlico. If he's supposed to think that and knows he's supposed to, then even Willi says to himself the sod must be in Camden Town – or German words to that effect. Okay?'

The houses backed on to their own gardens. They went out through the French windows that opened on to Flora's garden, an area that would have fascinated any collector of London weeds. He helped her over the wall into the garden opposite then forced the door in the side passage letting out on to the street.

He hailed a taxi and told the driver to take them to Pimlico. In twenty minutes they were in the white BMW, their suitcases already in the boot, and were crossing the Thames over Vauxhall Bridge, watching for the signs to Dover.

10

Drac stood in the midst of the umbrella pines that surrounded his house and listened to the night. In the distance he could hear the traffic on the Cogolin–Hyères road, but that was all. The silence still made him feel uneasy after years of living with background noises – doors clanging, key chains tinkling, men slopping out, men shouting, men dreaming aloud, men whispering, men farting. Here there was nothing.

Then, abruptly and frighteningly, the silence was broken . . . not by keys or doors, but by the noise of a chain dragging on the ground. It took him a moment to realise that it was only the dog moving its position.

He had a pencil torch in his pocket but he told himself he would not use it until he had to. He had been over this area during the day, now he must find his way in the dark.

He had had a couple of *fines* at the *bar-tabac* in La Motte, making them last an hour or more. He'd wanted another, he had had the taste, he could have gone on, but he had told himself, not here, not now. There would be plenty of time to get drunk.

The moon had not risen yet and the darkness was thick and cold. There would be frost soon and the dog's water would probably be frozen in the morning. Let's go, he thought.

He began to walk through the trees and in a few moments came to the wall. It was built of brick. Only a *rosbif* would have used brick when there was good mountain stone available.

He turned left along the wall, pushing through the undergrowth until he came to the rocks. He'd been astonished to discover they were still in place. He had put them there himself more than twenty years before. The police hadn't bothered to move them. Maybe they didn't think it was their business.

Now they were overgrown with shrubbery and grasses and lichens so that they looked as though they had been there since the world began.

He stopped and listened once more. No sounds. He placed his right foot on the biggest rock and his hands on the top of the wall and heaved himself up so that he lay on the top on his belly. In the old days he'd been able to go over in one movement, even holding the gun.

With his legs hanging over the far side his feet felt for the rocks that formed the other part of his own personal ladder.

He could feel a shrub, then something solid. He allowed his weight to come down on his foot. He was on the top of the inner rocks. He lowered himself to the ground.

As though to welcome him to land that had once been his father's and now should by rights have been his, the moon lipped the horizon and the house and gardens were bathed in silver.

The place was not quite as he remembered it, there seemed to be many more trees and shrubs. Had they taken an interest in the garden? In the *bar-tabac* they had said that only one of the daughters ever came.

He moved from shadow to shadow. It was all so familiar and yet so strange. Of course he was thinking of the garden in its early days with young trees and young shrubs. Everything had grown up, just like the girls. The lime tree had become even bigger and there were cedars that were now level with the roof. A clump of mimosas had seeded themselves and grown into a wild tangle.

The house was shuttered and still. It was built in an L-shape with a swimming pool in the L. He walked to it, and looked down. In the moonlight he could see that it was empty. Leaves had gathered and grass was growing up through the joints of the coping stones and flags. The stainless steel ladder glowed in the moonlight.

Between the pool and the house was the terrace of red brick. That was where the gas barbecue had stood, and where there had been a round white table and several chairs and a couple of loungers.

Before the wall had been built he used to walk across the property with his shotgun on his shoulder, showing that here he could go where he liked, do what he liked, and sometimes he had seen the *rosbif* sitting out by the pool in the shade of an umbrella, tapping away on a typewriter.

Once, for the hell of it, he had shot a blackbird which had a nest in the garden. That had driven the Englishman wild. He had come yelling and waving his arms, but Drac had picked up the bird and put it in his game bag and had laughed at him and told him to stick his head up his arse. Of course Fleming called the police and there had been a row – the first of many.

The house was double-storeyed and had been built like a Provençal farmhouse with solid wooden shutters covering the windows, fastened from the inside. He wandered round, looking for a broken shutter or where a knot had come out of the wood so that he could shine his torch into the rooms, but everything was closed tight. That was a pity because he did not know the lay-out of the house and knowledge like that might be important.

He crossed the drive and stood for some moments in the darkness by the side of the garage. Then he moved on to the big lime tree. One of the girls had had a swing in the tree, he recalled that she had played there often. She had always been by herself and had looked lonely.

He paused. This was the position from where he had seen them. He allowed the memories of that day, memories which he had so rigorously excluded from his thoughts in prison, to come back. He tasted them. They were bitter. He felt the anger stir in him again. He remembered standing here watching them come out of the pool, both of them naked. It had been hot that day, a real summer scorcher. Yvette's body he remembered most clearly for it was the last time he had seen it.

She would have been thirty then with heavy thighs and buttocks and big jutting breasts. That was how he liked his women: fleshy.

She had been dark, like a gypsy, with a mane of black-red hair, wet from the pool and glistening in the sunshine. He could see her now putting both hands up and squeezing it, her head cocked to one side. The *rosbif* had come out of the water after her. He must have been in his forties. Not much to look at. Scrawny. Already somewhat bald.

That's what had started the serious anger. The thought of her wanting to be naked with someone like the Englishman, yet if he, Drac, had asked her to take off her clothes and walk out of the house into the pine woods she would have laughed at him. What the hell had been in her mind? Did she think the Englishman was going to marry her?

They had taken the mattresses from the loungers and put them in the shade of the house and she had fetched a couple of drinks and they had lain down together and Drac had stood where he was now, hidden by the branches of the lime tree, and watched, and his hands had grown slippery on the gun.

The technicolour of his memories, the brightness of that day, the heat, the sunshine, the brilliant blue sky, faded into the present chiaroscuro and he found himself looking again at the moonlit terrace and the empty pool.

This time the anger spurted uncontrollably. He turned away, climbed the wall and went back to his house.

The dog growled.

'Don't be a fool,' he said. 'It's me.'

Still full of bitterness and anger, he opened a bottle of brandy and took a long drink. He was about to have a second when a warning voice again told him not to drink heavily. Not at this time of night. If he wanted to get drunk he must do so at ten o'clock in the morning or three o'clock in the afternoon. The night was too dangerous.

He went to bed and lay awake for a long time, and finally he slept.

The meal was over. Dubois and his wife were at their coffee and each was drinking a glass of Gran Marnier (the Huysmans of Belgium). The debris of the meal was all about them, the shells of four dozen Belon oysters, the remains of a *filet de boeuf,* a few remaining *frites.* Josephine took Toutou from her lap and placed him on the table. 'There, darling.'

Toutou sniffed the oyster shells and turned his nose up at the scraps of remaining meat, then wandered about the crockery looking pained.

They had not spoken a word during the meal but had addressed the food with the concentration it deserved. Now, as Dubois sat back, picked his teeth and lit a cigarette, he said, 'I wish he'd died in gaol.'

'Who?'

'Drac.'

She lifted Toutou and gave him a chocolate (Madame Rival) then, talking to the dog, she said, 'He musn't let the man get him down, must he?'

'I had a good look at that house when I saw him this morning. It's not bad. Solid. Heavy stones. Beams

I should think on the ground floor. Three bedrooms. You could do something with a place like that.'

'Toutou, what can he be thinking of?'

'I'm thinking why should we let developers come in here from the north and buy the land and put up houses for foreigners? Why can't we develop our own patch? You take someone like Drac. He must be hard up. How's he going to maintain himself? How's he going to live? Who'll give him a job? Even if he wasn't a gaol-bird, he's too old. So what can he do? Nothing. Now if a person made him the right offer, say enough to put down on a small apartment somewhere, you know the sort of thing, one room behind Toulon. Then, with what he gets from social security, he's got a nest egg and life's not so bad.'

'Then whoever bought his house could do it up and sell it,' Josephine said to Toutou.

'To foreigners.'

'Isn't papa clever? But he may not want to sell.'

'I thought of that. But there are ways. If your life becomes hard in one place you like to go somewhere else.'

'Toutou says, what sort of "hard"?'

'Let us say there was a policeman who did not like murderers, who wanted to keep things calm, who did his duty to the limit. There are pressures he could bring to bear. I hear he bought a car today. He used to drink like a fish, so they tell me. Car and drink. Every time he goes near a bar this policeman would test for alcohol, would demand his papers, would demand that he had the car checked for safety. There are many ways. So maybe he becomes glad to sell.'

'But not to the policeman who has been harassing him,' she said. 'Surely not.'

'The policeman's agent.'

'Aah,' she said.

He filled their glasses and picked them up. 'Shall we go?'

She smiled, slightly drunkenly, at him and he followed her into the bedroom.

They were undressing when the phone rang. 'Shit,' he said. 'It always happens, doesn't it?' He picked up the receiver. 'Yes?'

'It is Julien.'

'Who?'

'Julien at La Corniche in La Motte. You told me to ring if he came in.'

'Oh, yes, I'm sorry.'

'He was here for two hours. Drank two *fines*. I could go broke that way.'

'Did he make himself known?'

'Yes, but he didn't talk much. Just asked a few questions.'

'What sort of questions?'

'About the village. What happened to so-and-so. That sort. Most had died or gone away. Then he sat against the wall by himself. I suppose he was listening.'

'What did he hear?'

'I dunno. The bar was full. I was working my arse off.'

'Did anyone talk about the murder or the *rosbif* or the trial or anything to do with it?'

'Maybe, I can't say.'

'All right, Julien. Keep your ears open. And thanks.'

'What was that about?' Josephine said.

She was naked now, a mound of white shining flesh, her head on her arm, Toutou on her stomach. She was Jean-Claude's sex object, a policeman's *Maja Desnuda*. 'He's starting,' Dubois said, lifting the dog and placing it on its special cushion on the floor. 'He's playing games. He's like a woman showing a little bit of leg. He's showing them a little bit of himself.'

He finished undressing and lay beside her.

'You know,' she said thoughtfully. 'There are two houses.'

'What do you mean?

'The writer's house. What was his name?'

'Fleming.'

'Have you thought of that?'

'You mean buy it?'

'Either that or look after it like you look after the others.'

'I tried a couple of years ago. That daughter, what's her name, Flora. I spoke to her. She said she'd see. I've heard nothing since.'

He placed a hand absent-mindedly on one of her full white breasts. 'Security,' he said. 'It's all the rage now. I could have a good look at the house. Do a proper survey. See what its weak points are and then do a report for her. That means I'd have two strings to my bow.'

'That's brilliant, Jean-Claude.' She turned towards him. 'Toutou says it's time to stop talking.'

'One day I'll be able to leave the bloody poli— Aaah . . .'

'Is that nice, *chéri*?'

11

Jo had not realised how alone and vulnerable she had felt until she set off the following morning with the silver-grey Saab as running mate. Roger drove ahead and kept his speed down to about seventy. She followed at a distance of a few hundred metres.

The autoroute to Toulouse on a winter's day was almost deserted. It took long, lazy sweeps and at times she could see no other cars ahead or behind them.

The vicuña still bobbed on its elastic in front of her. She had grown to hate it as an artefact and for what it represented. But she played her tapes and found that she was no longer lonely.

They swung west round Bordeaux. Clouds the colour of liquid lead were coming in from the Atlantic. Occasionally a burst of rain would hit the windscreen.

Around the middle of the day, they came into heavy traffic on the Toulouse *périphérique,* but Roger drove in the slow lane and if she fell back he would let cars pass him and take up station in front of her once more.

All morning, on and off, she had been thinking of the house, and of the last time she had been there with her grandmother. She had been a teenager then, and she had hated and feared it – and so had the old lady, for she had said, 'I'm not sleeping here, Jo. Nothing in God's earth will get me to do that.'

They had gone to stay the night in St Tropez instead and looked over the house for wear and tear the following day with a builder from Cogolin in attendance. Even so Jo had been frightened, especially when they went near the swimming pool area.

She wished that Roger could be with her when she went to the house this time; just for an hour, even half an hour, at the beginning. But she knew it was impossible. The problem was that she would not get there until after dark. Maybe she should stay in a hotel tonight and go to the house in the morning. That was the sensible thing to do and to hell with Mike's phone call.

They were beyond Toulouse when she saw Roger's indicator signal that he was stopping. She joined him in a lay-by. He opened her passenger door and climbed in beside her.

'There's nowhere to eat around here,' he said. 'I've had another idea. I bought these quiches in Saintes this morning. Let's eat them for lunch and then we can have dinner together.' She felt a sudden lifting of her spirits. 'After that, you go on to La Motte and I go on to Cannes.' He showed her a vacuum flask. 'Coffee.'

'Fantastic!'

It was cold and blustery outside but the inside of the VW was warm and cosy. He looked at her tapes. 'Pink Floyd ... Brubeck ... Scarlatti ... Miles Davis ... Duruflé? I thought only Frenchmen knew Duruflé. I admire your taste.'

'Thank you.' She was pleased by the compliment. They ate the quiches and drank the coffee. 'What's that?' he said, pointing to the statuette.

'I don't really like things like that hanging in a car, but my husband put it there for luck.' She knew it sounded lame.

'Do you believe in luck.'

'I suppose so. Anyway, I touch wood. Do you?'

'Not really.' There was a sudden bleakness in his voice that matched the weather.

They drove all afternoon, picking up heavy lorry traffic from Spain around Montpellier. Darkness came and with it a driving rain. Clack . . . clack . . . went the wipers . . . lights came out of the darkness at her . . . cars passed . . . huge trucks sent up spray that almost blinded her . . . but always, just when she thought she had lost him, the friendly rear lights of the Saab appeared in front of her like some beacon telling her that all was well, that she was not alone. They left the rain behind at Aix.

They stopped in Cogolin about nine and parked in the small square. The sky was clear and the moon shone. It was very cold.

A restaurant called *Le Matelot* had a string of lights above its terrace. Inside there were fishing nets and green glass fishing floats, sailor hats, and a tank full of fish. The place was half full.

'I hope the food is edible,' he said.

'Well, it's cheerful. It's the sort of place you want to find at the end of a long day's drive.'

They ordered fish soup with *rouille*, then the *gigot* with *flageolets*.

He studied the wine list. 'I think something with body, don't you?' He ordered a bottle of Hermitage.

'Is your husband superstitious?' he said.

The change of subject confused her for a moment. 'My husband? No, not . . . oh, the thing in the car. Yes . . . sometimes.'

'Not always, but sometimes.'

She smiled. 'I suppose so.'

'Where you are concerned. I don't blame him. Tell me about him.'

'Mike?'

'If that is his name. Yes, Mike.'

'I don't—'

'We talked about ourselves last night. We mustn't be selfish.'

'Well, he's tall and big and good-looking – at least I think so.'

'How old?'

'Thirty-three.'

'And what does he do?'

'He deals in antiques.'

'How did you meet?'

'I was in rep with the Horseshoe in Basingstoke. We were doing an Ayckbourn. He came round afterwards. A friend of a friend. We had a drink together, then a Chinese meal. That's how it started.'

'And he was in antiques then?'

'In a small way. He was in the Army before that.'

'What regiment?'

'Royal Hampshire Fusiliers. He'd been in Germany with NATO.'

'Where was he stationed?'

'Near the Dutch border, I think.'

'What rank?'

'Captain.'

'You like the soup?'

'It's marvellous.'

'It's good that we're both eating it.'

'My grandmother used to eat garlic for colds.'

'Was it his first marriage?'

'Who? Mike?' She smiled. 'Why do you ask?'

'He's in his thirties. If you are going to get married, maybe you do it earlier.'

'I told you, he was in the army.'

'Soldiers do not marry?'

'It was his first and my first.'

'Of course. How old are you?'

'Twenty-seven. I told you last night.'

'You look seventeen, maybe a year more.'

'You make me sound like a child bride.'

The *gigot* and the Hermitage were served.

'This . . . antiques business. He's away a lot, your Mike?'

'Quite a lot.'

'Where does he go?'

'Scotland, the North.'

'And Europe?'

His eyes were fixed on her face. The stare made her uncomfortable. She had thought of asking him to come with her to the house but now she decided against it and returned to her original idea of going to a hotel.

'Yes. Sometimes.'

'Whereabouts?'

'Vienna. He buys at the State auction house, the Dorotheum. Not antiques really, but *bibelots*.'

'What sort?'

The questions were coming one on top of the other. It wasn't like last night. That had been slow and lazy and amusing. She felt now that she was being battered by questions. His voice had become as cold as his eyes. The fun had gone from the evening.

'What sort?' he repeated.

She felt irritated. 'Does it matter?'

'I must know about my opposition.'

'Your *what?*'

'When I get back to London, I am going to telephone you. We are going to have a liaison.'

She tried to smile but her lips were stiff.

'The English do not like to be told things like that,' he said. 'They do them, but they do not like to mention them. It is not "done". In France we are more honest. So I tell you. You have a man who leaves you alone and this is bad. You live in Pimlico and I live just over the river. When he goes to Scotland or to Vienna you will pick up the telephone and, *voila,* you are no longer alone. Don't you think it is a good idea?'

'And you'll become my Mr Whoozit.'

85

'Mr . . . ?'

'Private joke.'

She thought of Mike, big and heavy, and this slender, thin-faced man. They could not have been more different. She wanted to make a joke of it, keep things light, but Roger had spoken with an intensity that made her uncomfortable.

She looked at her watch. It was nearly ten-thirty. The owner cleared their plates and she asked him if there was a hotel nearby. He pointed across the square to the Prince de Galles. At this time of the year there would always be rooms, he said.

'So you are not going to the house tonight?'

'I don't like strange houses in the dark.'

'Strange?'

'I haven't been there for years.'

They ordered coffee. He felt in his pockets, then he said, 'Excuse me, I must get some cigarettes from the car.'

She was sitting facing the square and she watched him go out through the big glass doors on to the brightly lit terrace. He walked quickly and purposefully. She wondered what it would be like to have a 'liaison' with someone like him. She had not had an affair since she'd been married though there had been plenty of opportunities. She didn't know about Mike. Right at the beginning he had talked about an 'open' marriage. She assumed that he meant what most men meant, open for him, and supposed that on his trips . . . She saw Roger go to the back of the Saab and raise the hatch. He pulled out a jacket and began to search the pockets. And then she felt her scalp prickle. It wasn't a jacket. Quite clearly in the lights from the terrace she saw that it was a red and white parka.

She *had* been right! She *had* seen him before! He was the man who had been watching her at the market, pretending to take photographs.

Why? Why? Why?

Suddenly it was all plain. He must have been with Willi. They'd taken it in turns to watch her.

The VW was next to the Saab and she could see the small statuette hanging from the mirror. Is that what he wanted? If he knew what it was he could have taken it last night or on the road near Toulouse . . . or, wait . . . maybe he had decided that it was better to let her carry it. It was safe where it was. But safe from whom?

My God, what if Roger had followed her to look after their interests while Willi dealt with Mike? What a *fool* she'd been. She had to get away. She had to get to the house. She'd be safe there. Mike would phone and she could warn him. He would know what to do.

Roger was coming back. The coffee arrived. She rose, 'I must go to the loo.' He was sitting with his back to the window. She crossed the restaurant, moving out of his sight and then, instead of going through the door next to the small bar, she went quickly into the road.

She looked back once. Roger was pouring the coffee. She got into the VW. It was on a downward slope. She let off the hand brake and free-wheeled to the bottom of the square, then she started the engine and drove through the small narrow streets, not knowing where she was heading, just getting out of town.

She drove furiously and it was only when she reached a dark, heavily-wooded area that she realised she had been driving without lights. She put them on and saw she was on a small country road. She had no idea where she was heading nor had she any sense of direction.

A turning loomed and she took it, but this was an even smaller road so she wrenched the VW round. She drove on and on into seemingly deeper and more lonely countryside, for the road began to twist and turn as it wound into hills. Finally, she stopped. She consulted her map. She must be driving directly into the Massif des Maures, in precisely the opposite direction from the one she wanted.

She doubled back, side roads loomed up, but she decided to stay with the one she was on. Eventually she came to a cross-road. She realised she had been driving for nearly an hour. A sign said St Tropez, another pointed in the direction of Hyères, a third back to Cogolin. She put on the light and looked at her map. She thought she knew vaguely where she was, and turned on to the Hyères road. Soon it joined a larger road. There were the occasional lights of a car. Then she saw the sign: LA MOTTE.

She put her foot down and soon had the VW racing along at nearly seventy. She could not go fast enough. The house, which had for so long been a place of terror in her mind, had now taken the aura of a sanctuary. She wanted to close the door, wrap the house around her, and talk to Mike.

Suddenly the sign Route du Canadel showed in her lights. She swung the VW up the narrow, bushed lane. Her headlights bored into the tunnel of dusty green. She knew that the house was somewhere up on her right. Its shape and colour and position were etched deeply into her mind.

She was bouncing and banging along the pot-holed road when she swung round a corner and there, blocking her path, was a car, side on to her. She slammed on the brakes. The wheels locked and on the loose surface of the road the VW sailed on out of control. There was a grinding crash. She was flung forward, held by the seatbelt. The VW spun, teetered, then righted itself, facing the way it had come. She sat rigid, her hands, gripping the wheel, were like talons.

In her headlights she could see the car plainly. It was the silver-grey Saab and it was lying on its side in a vineyard. Roger was hanging in his seat belt, his head against the window.

Panic gripped her. She backed the VW, made a spurting turn and fled the place.

The house came up within a minute, the gates to her right. She leapt out of the van, opened them, drove through. In a shower of gravel she stopped near the front door, unlocked it and felt for the light switch. Nothing happened.

Panic seized her again. 'Stop it!' she told herself. 'Think!'

She ran out to the VW and brought back a torch. She entered the house through the huge living-room. The furniture was covered in dust sheets. The kitchen was off a passage to the left. She remembered there was a boiler room off the kitchen. She opened its door and shone the torch around the walls. The fuse box was above the door. She pulled the main switch, something clicked beside her and made her jump. Then she realised it was the fridge switching itself on.

She went round the ground floor switching on lights. She fetched her case and then locked the door behind her. Only then did the panic begin to subside.

The noise of the crash woke Drac. He did not know that there had been a crash, only that something had woken him. He lay listening to the silence, then he heard something he could identify: a low whining.

The dog had water, it had been fed. Why? Then came a different sound, of movement within the house itself. Someone was in his living-room.

Quietly, he got out of bed, took the coarse blanket under which he had been sleeping and hung it over the small window, blotting out the moonlight.

He felt for his knife under the bolster but even as he did so he realised it was too fierce a weapon. He knew that he would not be forgiven even if it was an intruder against whom he used it, Dubois would see to that.

There was a large porcelain jug on the old-fashioned wash-stand, but that also might be too much. There were only his hands, but he must be careful with these. A man had died when he'd used his hands.

He heard a creak on the stairs. There were two other bedrooms. The latch of the second one clicked and the door opened as whoever it was inspected it. After a few moments muffled footsteps came along the uncarpeted boards towards his room. He heard whispering: there had to be two of them.

He stood behind the door. The first man entered. There was a glint of light on the barrel of a shotgun. Drac grabbed the barrel and jerked the man into the room, slamming the door with his foot. They struggled for a moment, then, with one of his huge hands balled into a fist, he hit the man on the side of the head. He went down as though clubbed by an axe. As he fell Drac heard the running footsteps of the other going down the stairs.

Drac lit his candle and studied the man. He was one of the gypsies from whom he had bought the dog.

'I've been expecting you,' he said. He placed the gun under his bed, knowing he would have to find a place to hide it later. Then he put the gypsy on his shoulder and took him down through the pines and dumped him near the road.

He crouched there for a moment, watching the man return to consciousness then he said softly, 'Come back and I will break your knees.' He went back to the house.

In the pines, the second gypsy, the one who had run for it, joined the injured man. 'You all right?' The other did not reply. 'Let's get out of here.'

'The gun.'

'Forget the gun. He's like a wild bull, that one.'

He helped the man to his feet and they went off

down the road. They had not gone more than a few hundred yards when they saw the Saab.

They approached it warily. It was canted over on a slight slope. The two of them managed to right it. They opened the driver's door and pulled the unconscious figure of Roger out on to the ground.

They opened the hatch, took out his suitcase and went through his belongings. They noted that there were several items they could easily sell: the parka, a clock radio, a jersey, a typewriter and a camera. There was also a small pistol. But the prize was the car. They knew a place in Nice where expensive foreign cars were always in demand. A new set of papers, new plates, a panel-beating job and a respray and you could sell a car like this for good money in Belgium.

The ground was hard and frosty, the Saab was front-wheel drive. At first the wheels spun, then they gripped, and in a moment it was back on the road.

The car was almost new. The man who had run turned to the other. 'Was it worth it?'

'Was what worth it?'

'Your headache.'

'Don't talk. Drive.'

12

Jo hurried from room to room putting on lights. She did not look around and tried to keep her mind a blank. She wanted the house illuminated before she placed herself in it. Finally, she stood in the middle of the living-room and said out loud, 'Okay, I'm here.'

It wasn't as she remembered it. When she had been there with her grandmother the light in the far corner had been orange. But, of course, the sun had been out then, streaming through the windows. Now the shutters were tight and the red-tiled floor absorbed what light there was.

The room was freezing. She made herself go into the boiler room in its dark little passage off the kitchen. She had hated the room when she and her grandmother had visited the house. 'Just the place for mice and rats,' Mrs Byron had said. 'Ugh! It gives mee the creeps!'

Jo thought she remembered a large wall cupboard but she must have been mistaken for the heaters were in an old chest that sat on the floor opposite the boiler.

She took them back into the living-room and switched them on. They matched the house. The furniture and the appliances were all getting on: the old-fashioned water-heater in the bathroom, the fridge that sounded like a motor-cycle as it shuddered into life, the wooden draining board, the yellowing bath. It reminded her of a stage set of *Look Back in Anger*.

As far as she could see Flora hadn't spent a penny on

the place since their father died. It was a museum piece. Post-war Provençal. All it needed was a *traction avant* in the drive outside.

While she was examining the house, part of her mind was listening for the telephone. It sat on a small table in the sitting-room, a heavy black instrument. After a while she picked it up and listened to the humming French dialling tone. It was working, thank God.

She stood in front of one of the heaters rubbing her frozen hands. 'Okay . . . okay . . .' she said to herself. What to do about Roger? She had simply been putting things off and she couldn't put them off any longer.

She sat down on one of the dust-sheeted chairs. She couldn't just leave him. Or could she? This is what she needed Mike to tell her. Mike would know. Then she thought, perhaps he had already phoned.

She found the code and dialled Flora's number. 'Come on . . . Come on . . . !'

But it went on ringing. Was she with Mr Whoozit? Was she off somewhere, bonking?

If this was England she would dial 999 and say, 'There has been an accident on the Canadel Road. You will find a grey Saab on its roof in a vineyard.'

And when they said, 'What is your name?' she would hang up, knowing they'd never trace her but also knowing she had done what she could.

But here? In French? If she phoned the police they'd know from her accent that she was English. The car was near the house owned by English people. Wouldn't they come here first and find the VW?

But what if he bled to death, was bleeding to death right now, while she was switching on lights and listening to the fridge and ringing London?

In her mind was a movie image she had seen several times of a World War I pilot in a crashed plane. They had filmed him hanging upside down from his straps, blood dripping on to the ground from his shattered skull.

You wouldn't even let a criminal die that way, she thought.

But if she did go to the police, how would she explain what had happened? Maybe she wouldn't have to. She'd been coming to her house and hit the car, which was trying to turn on the narrow road. Simple.

And better not phone. Go in person. There must be a police station in La Motte.

But what if they asked why she had waited half an hour?

Shock. Trauma. Yes, trauma. That was a good word.

She went out, locked the door and got into the van. She wouldn't have to stop at the car. Go right past. Get the police. Already the beginning of the conversation was going though her mind: *Excusez moi, m'sieu* . . .

She drove back down the road. Her lights bored through the darkness illuminating trees and bushes. She came to the corner, slowed and pointed the lights to illuminate the Saab. It wasn't there. She could have sworn this was the place. She went on slowly. She could see nothing.

She backed up to the original corner. It had to be this one. There on the road were her skid marks. But where was the Saab?

You leave a car upside down with the driver hanging by his safety straps, you come back and there's nothing. No car. No man.

He must have come round and managed to get out. What then? He would have walked down to the main road. It wasn't more than half a kilometre. He could have flagged down a car, asked for help.

She could see in her mind's eye the whole scene: several powerful French farmers heaving the car right-side-up and then pushing it out on to the road.

And he'd gone! Driven off!

She offered up a silent prayer to whichever of the

Gods was responsible for luck. She turned the VW and drove back to the house.

Then she thought: what if he has gone to the police to report the accident? But he wouldn't, would he? He wouldn't want to have to explain, wouldn't want them to start investigating.

It was more likely that he had gone to a hospital. His treatment there could take hours. She was probably safe until tomorrow and by then . . . by then Mike would surely have phoned.

She parked the VW out of sight of the road because she didn't want anyone to see the dents in its front, and walked round the house to the door. Above the sound of her feet on the gravel she heard something else. It was the phone.

She ran, fumbling for the keys, managed to fit one, tore the door open and raced into the house. As she put her hand on the receiver, the ringing stopped.

'Mike! Oh Mike!'

Her body was trembling, her hand shaking.

'Oh Mike, just one more ring!'

And then she thought: what if he was at home?

She dialled her own number in London. She could see the sitting-room, the phone by the door. She could hear it ringing in her house . . . her home . . . God, she wanted so desperately to be there!

The receiver was picked up. 'Hello.'

'Thank God you're—'

'Mick is not here,' the voice said and the connection was cut.

She stood staring at the instrument. Willi! It had been Willi!

'Oh, my God,' she said out loud.

A sound seemed to answer. She turned. In the open doorway stood a figure. It was so covered in dirt and blood as to be almost unrecognisable. It took two steps into the room.

She wanted to scream. To throw something. Instead she watched as a rabbit watches a snake. Another step. Then slowly, like a tree falling, Roger toppled over on to the floor.

She looked down at him and gradually the terror left her. One side of his face and head was covered in a poultice of black earth and blood. What should she do? The police? She dismissed that instantly.

But she had to do something. It was now she needed to talk to someone: her grandmother, Flora, Mike. None available.

So talk to yourself, she thought.

Alternatives, not counting the police. Get out of the house, go to a hotel and leave him. Or drag him out, lock the door and stay inside.

Both were silly. He could be dying and she was the cause of it.

'Right,' she said out loud. 'You're an actress, so act. The part calls for someone who can control her emotions in a tight corner and who is a competent nurse . . .'

The water in the taps was still only lukewarm. She lit the Calor gas stove and put on a big pot of water, then she fetched blankets from the cupboard upstairs and a couple of pillows. She found an old fan heater and switched that on.

She began to undress him. The coat and trousers came off easily enough but his shirt and underwear were stuck to his body. She used the warm water to soften the dried blood and eventually managed to pull the fabric away.

She found towels and began to wash him.

His body was white and slender. He looked innocent lying there and she thought: how could you tell a criminal without his clothes on? He wasn't even wearing the gold chain or bracelets that were supposed to be de rigueur for TV mobsters.

When she had finished she stripped the cushions from

the sofa, pushed them underneath him, wrapped him in blankets then sat down in one of the big armchairs and took the cigarette packet from the pocket of his jacket. She lit herself one for the first time in two and a half years.

She didn't know how badly he was hurt. On the surface there were bruises and abrasions but she could not tell what internal injuries he might have suffered.

She double-locked the door, then curled up again in her chair. She wanted to keep an eye on him in the bright electric light.

Seeing him naked had, in some strange way, partially allayed her fear of him. She had gone through his clothes: there was no gun, no knife. He did not look the criminal type, but who knew what the type looked like, anyway?

She hadn't any idea what she was going to do with him, or with herself, for that matter. But Mike was probably on his way now.

Then she remembered Willi. He must be looking for the vicuña.

She suddenly felt a bitter anger. How the hell had she got into a mess like this? Some Austrian was breaking up her house in London, looking for something she hadn't even known existed, and here in France she was cooped up with a Frenchman who wanted the same thing.

But if Willi and Roger were partners, why was Willi at the house? And why hadn't Roger simply taken the little animal? All he had needed to do was break the elastic and say thank you very much.

She went into the kitchen and looked round for a weapon. She didn't like knives, didn't think she'd ever have the courage to use one. She found an old wooden meat mallet which her mother must have used to tenderise steak years and years before.

When she went back into the living-room Roger's eyes were flickering. He put a hand to his head, then held it

97

over his eyes to shield them from the bright lights.

'What happened?' he said.

'You had an accident.'

He tried to sit up. The pain in his head must have been severe for he held it with two hands, then lay back.

'Where are my clothes?'

'In the kitchen.'

'Did you undress me?'

'Yes.'

'Are you going to hit me with that?'

'Not if you behave.'

'I am in your house?'

'Yes.'

'I remember driving to your house, but no one was here. Why did you leave the restaurant? Did you think . . . ? You English women! You act like virgins even when you're not.'

'You've been following me.'

'Of course I have been following you.' He winced again. 'I told you I had been following you. I followed you from the moment the ferry reached France. Do you have a cigarette?'

'No, but you have.'

'Light it for me.'

She lit one for him and another for herself. 'I meant you were following me before we arrived in France. You were following me in London. I saw you at the Camden Lock Market. You were taking pictures.'

'When? When did you see me?'

'On Sunday. And the other man, Willi. I'd seen him, too.'

'Willi?'

'Don't pretend. The Austrian with the Tyrolean hat and the feather. Don't think I'm that stupid.'

He shook his head as though to clear it, and winced with pain. 'Please . . . Look, I was at the market. But why not? I am a journalist. I was doing a story about it.'

'Why were you taking pictures of me?'

'I swear to you on my mother's grave, I never saw you before the ferry.'

'Why did you come here, to the house?'

'I was worried about you. What would you have done if you were me? We are dining pleasantly. You walk out. After a while I go out and your bus is not there . . .'

'What did you think?'

'I thought, she's bored with me. But why? I am not boring. Maybe she is sick and has gone to her house. I was worried.'

'How did you find it?'

'That was not difficult. I went to the bar in La Motte. I said, which is the house belonging to the English people?'

'And then?'

'And then I drove up the road. The house was dark and empty. So I drove back but then I thought, maybe I'd better wait and see if you come.'

'How did you know I'd come?'

'I decided to wait for half an hour. I was turning in the road when some idiot hit me. I remember it rolling over into the vineyard. Then nothing.'

She opened her mouth, then closed it.

He went on, 'But when I came to the car was gone!'

13

When Willi Trott was a little boy his father had had a stall in the Volksprater amusement park in Vienna, selling *lingos,* the Hungarian snack of fried dough sprinkled with garlic. His father had always had great faith in garlic. He said it was like yoghurt. If you ate a lot of garlic or yoghurt, or both, you lived to be a hundred and ten.

Unfortunately, one night, full of schnapps, he had stepped in front of a tram going up the Döblingerhaupstrasse and the garlic hadn't saved him.

Willi ran the stall with his mother until her varicose veins became too bad to stand all day. Then he ran it by himself. Not during the day because he was at school, but at night.

There were others who wanted the pitch and Willi had to defend himself. First he learned to use a bicycle chain, then a club studied with nails.

In the Volksprater he was known as 'wild' Willi. At school he was known as 'neat' Willi because even then he always dressed well. When he was fifteen there was a pop song called 'In the Summertime' sung by Mungo Jerry. Willi loved that song. He sang it every day, long after it had dropped out of the charts. They started calling him 'Mungo Willi', until he broke a boy's finger on the slats of a wooden shower mat by hitting it with a hockey stick. When he grew up he lost his hair and was called 'bald' Willi – but not to his face.

He no longer had the *lingos* stand in the Volksprater, instead he thought of himself as an international businessman. He owned a house in Sievering and he was treasurer of the tennis club. He had two children at a private kindergarten in the Krottenbachstrasse.

Now, as he moved through Flora's dark apartment by the light of a pencil torch, he lived up to one of his nicknames. He worked neatly, picking up objects and examining them in the light of his torch and putting them back exactly where he had found them.

He went through drawers and her cupboards. He did not find anything, and the place looked as though it had already been picked over. There were empty hangers in the walk-in cupboard, the clothes drawers were half empty. The bed was unmade and rumpled, and that offended him.

He had also been offended at what he'd had to do at Mick's place. It had been against his nature. But it had to be done and, anyway, he hadn't broken anything. He'd placed the overturned chairs carefully on their sides. As he searched – he wasn't quite sure what he was looking for, but would know when he found it – his mind went over the evening.

Mick had said he would be here, but he wasn't. He hadn't been in Pimlico, either. So where the hell was he? He could feel the anger and resentment begin to eat into his soul.

At last, in the wastepaper basket in Flora's bedroom, he found a travel agent's receipt. He smoothed it out and read it by torchlight. It was for the one a.m. ferry from Dover to Boulogne.

They had taken off! Just like that! Who could you trust these days?

He sat on the bed and read the receipt through carefully. Driver; BMW car; one passenger. It was a one-way reservation.

Well, he had searched the house in Pimlico again, not more than an hour before, and he'd searched Flora's apartment. And when Willi searched he searched thoroughly as well as neatly.

He could only conclude that they had taken it. And that was very naughty. He began to nibble a hang-nail. But taken it where?

He had heard them talking about a house in France. That was probably where they were going. He knew they had decided to dump Mick's wife – had that been her on the phone? – though he could not imagine why. Who wanted to get into bed with a clothes hanger when you could cuddle up to a dumpling? Not that Mick's wife was round like a dumpling, but she was small and pretty and soft and golden and he felt he could have eaten her.

This was so ungrateful of Mick! After all Willi had done for him, even introducing him to Kleist and the boys.

He had been sitting in the dark for some minutes, smoking a cigarette and brooding about what he was going to do when he heard the street door open.

He rose from Flora's bed and stood behind the half-open bedroom door. Through the long vertical crack he saw a figure enter, lock the door behind him and switch on the hall lights. He was wearing a studded black leather jacket and a big black safety helmet with a tinted visor.

Willi watched as he took off the helmet and jacket and dropped them on the floor. He flicked on the lights in the sitting-room and went in. Willi followed him silently.

He was a small man in middle age with a full beard that was mainly grey. He helped himself to a cigarette and lit it. He looked around as though he owned the place.

'*Guten abend*,' Willi said.

The man turned in surprise, and Willi hit him. He sailed backwards, crashed into the low coffee table and collapsed on the white rug. Willi pulled up a chair and sat, looking down at him. In the movies Willi had seen people at this point take the flowers from a vase and throw water over an unconscious figure. This offended his sense of propriety. He did not want the beautiful white rug to get all wet. So he waited.

It took Harry Evans less than five minutes to sit up. He was groggy and held his jaw. He looked at Willi, blinking his eyes. Willi remained blurred for some moments and then swam into focus. Harry didn't much care for what he saw.

'Who're you?' he said.

'Who are you?' Willi replied.

'I asked first. This ain't your flat. I'm asking what you're doing here?'

'Is it yours?'

'No, but I got rights.'

He started to get up but Willi pushed him back with the point of his shoe. 'Be calm.'

'Calm!' There was a rising note of indignation. 'That's bloody marvellous, that is. Calm! I come here, within my rights, and suddenly biffo.'

'Biffo?'

'Listen,' Harry said, becoming confidential. 'This ain't my place. You want to do a little B and E be my guest. You let me out, you finish your business, I come back later.'

'B and E?'

'Breaking and entering. Burglary. Robbing. You foreign then?'

'Maybe.'

'Well, that's it, in't it? That's what it's all about these days. International. You rob us, we rob you. Fair's fair. So why don't I scarper for an hour? You take what you want . . . ' He began to rise again and again Willi pushed him back.

'I am not a robber,' Willi said.

'Oh, I get it. You thought *I* was breaking in. No, no, I'm looking after the place. I'm a friend.'

'Of Flora's?'

'That's it. Flora's. You a friend, too? Of course you are. That's all right then.'

'Where is Flora?'

'She split. She's gone.'

'To France,' Willi said, throwing the travel agency's receipt on to the floor.

Harry fumbled for his granny-glasses and looked at it. 'That's it. France.'

'Where in France?'

'You got me there, mate.'

Willi was having difficulty in understanding Harry. Perhaps it was his accent, he thought. But he also spoke very quickly. There was only one way to slow him down. He picked up a heavy glass ashtray from the coffee table and brought it down sharply on Harry's knee.

Harry fell back, shouting with pain. 'Jee-sus!' he said. 'What you do that for!'

'I look for Flora. Now. The house?'

Harry was rubbing his knee. 'She said I wasn't to give the address. She's only going to be there a few days and then . . . Africa. She's emigrating, see. That's what she says, anyway. Who knows?'

'The address,' Willi said, picking up the glass ashtray again.

'All right, mate, all right.' He pulled a small diary from his shirt pocket and paged through it. 'That's it,' he said.

Willi ripped the page out and threw the book back at him. He paused at the doorway. 'Have a nice night,' he said. Then he went into the street.

Drac lay awake for a long time after the gypsies had gone. He had hidden the shotgun and the cartridges and

104

then had stood near the dog. 'You didn't warn me they were coming,' he said. 'But I can understand. Next time, though.'

He went back to bed, feeling safer. He knew they would not come again.

The silence of the night was oppressive and he wondered if he would ever get used to it. He had bought a small radio and now he turned it on. He didn't care what it played as long as it made a noise.

Sometime later he thought he heard the sound of a car engine. He turned the radio down and listened. It was gone. Maybe it had been down near the little bridge. Probably someone taking a short cut across the Col du Canadel. He turned up the radio again and lay back.

The visit to the house had upset him. Seeing her body in his mind, the picture he had so ruthlessly rejected all these years, had stirred up his anger. Now the images crowded in from the periphery of his mind. He heard the two shots again and smelled the cordite and saw the blood and the bodies. God, there had been blood.

He remembered the *rosbif* falling into the pool and instantly the water had turned the colour of weak potassium permanganate.

He fought to blot out the images. He turned the radio up and put his hand over his eyes. When it came away it was wet with sweat even though the room was freezing.

14

It was three a.m. and Jo was curled up in one of the big armchairs she had known since she was a small child, with a blanket, smelling of lavender, wrapped around her. She had Roger's cigarettes and lighter and had been smoking almost continuously. The room or the chair or the smell of lavender kept pushing the past at her and she in turn pushed hard against the past, refusing it entry into her thoughts for, if that happened, she knew she would never last the night – not without running or breaking down or both.

She looked down at Roger, asleep on his bed of sofa cushions. His face was pale and his eyelids flickered every now and then as though he was dreaming. He looked even more innocent as he slept than he had when she had washed him. Children looked innocent when they slept. But adults? Mike didn't look anything other than Mike. His heavy face hardly seemed to relax and he had a habit of grinding his teeth – an anguished, violent sound.

She went over Roger's story in her mind. Why shouldn't he have been at Camden Lock taking photographs? Even at the time she had wondered if she was imagining things. She did have an over-active imagination. Maybe he had managed to get out of the car by himself and had been wandering around and someone had seen it – two or three people perhaps – and righted it and driven it away. Stolen it.

The thing was, if he was the vicuña-man he would have taken the statuette and gone. Unless . . . well, unless he wanted the vicuña *and* Jo. Why not? She knew she appealed to men. A little something on the side. That's how he might have thought of her.

There were areas where she believed him and areas where she was not so sure. Her problem was that she did not know what to do. You can't get in touch with the police, she said to herself. You can't get in touch with Mike. Why not go to a hotel and come back later?

But what about the Saab? What if the police had found it . . . ? This was another scenario . . . What if Roger, concussed and confused, had released himself from the car and wandered away into the scrub oak forest and a patrolling police car had found the Saab and towed it to Cogolin? They would see where it had been hit. And then if she went blundering about in her VW with dents in the front and grey paint scrapes all over it . . . no, she couldn't do that either.

The best thing would be to wait until Roger woke and try to establish whether his story was true. She *wanted* it to be true. She wanted and needed an ally and a friend. What she didn't want and need was another enemy, another complication.

Because she knew she was in the middle of a horrible mess. When she thought about the future her lower abdomen contracted in fear and misery.

For argument's sake, suppose everything went smoothly: Roger left on his legitimate journalistic business, Mike arrived, they took the vicuña and sold it to the Italian for half a million pounds. Just say it worked, even to having a baby later. Could she just forget about all this? Tell herself it hadn't happened?

She remembered the time she had shoplifted from Woolworths. She'd got away with a couple of handfuls of chocolates and no one had seen her. But that night in bed she had begun to have waking nightmares of the store detective's hand on her shoulder. Arrest. Trial. Her grandmother's disgrace.

This wasn't a handful of chocolates, it was a pre-Colombian statuette that was illegally in Europe. Her house had been vandalised and she had been forced to make this journey. Would Willi just go away once they had sold the vicuña? Was it just 'business' as Mike had said?

Or wouldn't she lie in bed at night worrying? And with a baby, wouldn't the worry be even greater? Every time she paid at a supermarket wouldn't she think: this is the money from the vicuña?

And then she thought of something. Roger was deeply asleep. She slipped out of her chair and went to his clothes, which she had folded and put in a pile on the table. His wallet was still in his inside jacket pocket. She took it back to her own chair and wrapped herself in the blanket again. First she looked at the plastic: Carte Bleue and American Express were both in his name. That didn't tell her a thing. Then his AFP press card. But people could have press cards made. Then a letter, from the Great Northern Telegraph Company Limited, giving him 'collect' facilities for all stories filed from Denmark to Paris or London. That reassured her somewhat although she had seen too many spy movies involving forged documents to be certain.

She remembered his conversation at dinner in Saintes. 'Joanna Townsend bracket twenty-seven unbracket ...' Criminals didn't talk that way. But who said journalists couldn't also be criminals? What if he had got on to the story of the missing vicuña and decided to cut himself in?

She pulled out a second letter. It was handwritten in French. Shamelessly she read it.

'Dear Roger', it said, 'I cannot talk any more. When I talk I cannot think and that makes talking impossible. I cannot find the words. So I am writing this down. I know it is a cliché, a Dear John letter, but that cannot be helped.

'Even though we have discussed it endlessly you still do not seem to understand how I feel. If it was only your work, that would be bad enough, but I could understand. But you are obsessed by this thing.

'Saturdays, Sundays, your days off . . . I never see you. How many times have we been out together this year? How many times have we been to dinner? I don't mean working dinners, I mean just the two of us together. So few I can hardly remember.

'And even when you are at home you are, so to speak, not at home. You are always in the room with that new toy of yours.

'Week after week, month after month, I sit in this flat looking out over Battersea Park. Do you think I like being alone?

'Justine is everything to you, I am nothing. I could even put up with that if you did not make it so obvious.

'By the time you read this I will be back in Paris. I should never have left.'

The signature was 'Marie-Claire'.

She replaced the cards and letters in his wallet and put it back in his jacket. What was this 'thing' he was obsessed about? The vicuña? And who was Justine? He had told her his wife had left him because they were childless and she hated London. Now there was another woman; another little something on the side.

She leaned her head back against the chair but as she tried to think of some subtle questions to ask Roger when he woke, she went out like a light, as a child does, from being wide awake to limp unconsciousness in two seconds flat.

The two gypsies had stopped at an all-night *routier* on the outskirts of Frèjus. The taller and swarthier of the two, the man who had sold the dog, was called Figeras. His partner was smaller, with greasy, slicked-back hair. He still had a headache from Drac's blow. His name was Espino.

It was a small place, near the autoroute interchange, and the two men were the only customers. They drank coffee and *marc* and argued in low voices about which route to take to Nice. The autoroute was faster but there were police patrols. The coast road was slower and you had to go through towns where a Saab was extremely visible.

The owner of the place, a small thin Algerian known to everyone as Moustafa, which was not his real name, sat behind the bar looking at the sports pages of *Nice-Matin*. He rose and went to the door. It was a cold bright starlit night. He stood there for a minute or two then returned to his place.

'Two more,' Figeras said.

Moustafa served the coffee and the brandies. 'Cold tonight,' he said. 'Where're you making for?'

'Mind your own business,' Espino said.

Jo woke slowly and heavily and for a moment, before she opened her eyes, had no idea where she was. She was freezing, for the blanket had fallen away during the hours she had slept. Then she remembered . . .

But the room was in darkness. She had left the lights on. She flicked the lighter and looked at her watch. Just past eight o'clock. Then her eye caught the rumpled blankets on the floor. Roger was not there. She got up and put on the lights. His clothes were no longer on the table.

Suddenly she was afraid, not of Roger, wherever he was, but of the house itself. The heavy wooden shutters kept the daylight from the room. Roof timbers creaked. A wind had come up and she could hear it sighing around the corners. It was as though the house was trying to speak, to tell her something.

She jumped out of the chair and looked around in panic. She wanted Roger back. Even lying on the cushions he had been company. The night, her thoughts, the hours together, had all created a different image of him. She had almost been at the point of accepting his own evaluation of himself. She felt bereft.

She ran to the front windows and opened the shutters. Daylight streamed into the room. Then she did the same in the kitchen.

Everything should have been more cheerful but it wasn't. The interior was dingy and the harsh light was cruel. The house had been neglected. There were cracks in the walls and loose tiles on the floor. In the kitchen old stains marked the walls, and the cooker, now that she could see it properly, was spotted by grease.

She went outside thinking he might be there, that he might have gone to the VW or into the road. But all she could see was the wind-tossed trees. The sky was a high uniform grey and the wind was cold and dry. She turned the corner of the house and something moved by the wall.

With relief, she called his name.

But there was nothing near the wall. Had it only been a branch of the old lime tree moving in the wind? As she looked at the tree something jolted in her head.

There it was. Freeze-framed. The child on the swing.

Little Miss Muffet sat on a tuffet, eating her curds and whey . . .

And then her father's voice from the terrace. 'Joanna, darling, I'm working out here. Can't you go up to your room and play?'

And in the room Flora. 'I don't want you here!'

'But daddy said—'

'I'm reading. Go and play somewhere else.'

The view cleared. There was only the lime tree and the wind. She shivered and went back into the house.

When would Mike get here, she wondered? And what was she going to do until he came?

Open up the rest of the house. Let the light in. Banish the dark.

And when he did arrive? They didn't *have* to carry out his plan. That was something that had been eating away at her, perhaps even as she slept. She didn't *have* to go on with this. Nor did Mike. They had enough money without doing squalid deals, without letting people like Willi into their lives. She began to feel somewhat better. She would talk to Mike, argue, convince him – and if she couldn't convince him then she would have to decide what she herself was going to do. Nobody could *make* her do anything.

She went upstairs and opened the shutters on the landing then found herself in the top corridor. There were four rooms here besides the two bathrooms: the big bedroom which her mother and father had shared, the spare room into which her mother had moved just before she died. There was the room which Flora and Jo had shared and, at the end of the corridor, her father's study.

She opened the shutters in her parents' room. This side of the house overlooked a small pine wood. Was this where the man had come from? The one . . . ? Somewhere in the dim recesses of her memory she thought there might be a house hidden in the woods. She hurriedly turned back to the room. The old yellow candlewick spread was still on the bed. She supposed this was the room Flora used when she came down with all the Mr Whoozits of former years. She'd made no secret of the fact that she brought men here. Why shouldn't she?

No one would come to a place like this on her own.

Did she remember, or was it just that she *ought* to remember, climbing into this bed and being cuddled by her mother? It was the sort of thing all small children did. But the exact picture eluded her.

She opened the shutters in the rooms she and Flora had shared after moving from their original bedroom then went to her father's study. It was looking neglected. Books, papers, files, an old Remington typewriter, a gas heater, a writing table, a cane chair. Dust everywhere. Even sand blown through the cracks by twenty years of mistrals.

Now at the end of the corridor the last bedroom, the spare room. She opened the door. It smelled strongly of lavender.

She opened the door of what had originally been a walk-in closet but had then become the toy cupboard. This had been her sanctuary, her hide-away, her place of safety when Flora became vindictive. It had a light and also a lock which she had been able to operate from the inside and so was able to shut herself away for hours to draw or play.

It seemed much smaller now, but then the whole place seemed smaller. There was nothing in it now except her old panda.

It was the biggest they could buy at the time. She had carried it everywhere. Then her father had accidentally burned its forehead with a cigarette and her mother had put on a red flannel bandage. The bandage was still there giving the toy the appearance of a war casualty. Flora had tried to take her Panda away, even though she was too old for pandas. Maybe that's why she had carried it round with her all the time.

They were lying in bed, the lights were out and Flora was talking about the big spider.

113

'I don't want you to tell me!' Jo was saying.

'I'm not telling you.'

'You are! You're frightening me!'

'There's no law that says I can't talk out loud. Daddy says it's a free country.'

The story was about the big spider that lived in the pine forest.

'. . . and one day the little girl got lost in the forest and the big spider carried her off to his cottage . . .'

'I'm going to tell daddy! He'll punish you!'

'Daddy's little girl . . .' She began to chant, making a kind of song out of it. 'Daddy's little girl . . . daddy's little girl . . .' she said it over and over—

There was someone in the room, someone behind her. She whirled.

Roger stood there. He was dressed. His hair was combed. He carried a baguette, a pot of jam and a packet of coffee.

'Good morning,' he said. 'Breakfast?'

114

15

'Crisp,' Mike Townsend said to the waiter.

'M'sieu?' The waiter was not more than fifteen, with the bright red cheeks of Normandy. He was nervous.

'Jesus! The bacon. I want it crisp.'

'*Bien cuit,*' Flora said.

The boy turned away, still puzzled.

They were in the dining-room of the Hôtel Versailles in Vienne, their table in the big window overlooking the swirling, grey-green waters of the Rhône and the rush-hour traffic on the quay.

'There's one thing I can do without,' Flora said.

'What's that?'

'You being rude to waiters.'

His face darkened with anger and she covered his hand with hers. 'Don't be macho, darling. Not here. In a little while. Up in the room. Then you can be anything you want.'

She was a different Flora now. Her make-up, which she had checked regularly on the Channel crossing and at intervals on the journey south when they stopped for coffee at the cafés on the autoroute, was still in place. Her lips were a red slash, the make-up round her eyes startling in the cold light that came in through the windows. There were hollows under her eyes and her face was even more angular. There was a hard, brittle, brilliant quality about her; diamondiferous, crystalline.

They were both tired. The crossing had been too

short to sleep, too long to keep awake. Then had come the long drive south of Paris in the early hours to pick up the autoroute. He had driven fast. She liked to watch him. He was a good driver. He'd once won the army sports car championship. His only problem was that he had to pass everything on the road.

Their breakfasts arrived. He was having the 'English' breakfast, she the Continental.

'I told you,' he said, turning the bacon over with a fork. 'All bloody grease. They haven't a clue.'

The head waiter was making his rounds. *'Tout va bien, m'sieu?'* Mike glowered at him.

'Oui, merci,' Flora said. Then, as the waiter nodded and turned away, she said to Mike, 'For Christ's sake, we're both tired. Don't make things harder.'

He nodded. 'Sorry. I'm never good in the mornings.'

'Those are just the things we have to know about each other, sweetie, if we're going to live together.'

They had taken a room, planning to sleep and continue their journey later in the day. But Flora had no intention of going to sleep immediately. Once they were in bed she became soft, pliable, twining round him like some jungle vine, working for her pleasure, making it last, exhausting both of them in a different way.

Her moods were bewildering, he thought. One minute the tough cookie, the next the mistress, with a sexual appetite like a rutting stag. He'd have to get used to these changes in moods.

When they were done she rose and looked for cigarettes, her thin figure with the small, almost juvenile, breasts, passing back and forth before the windows as though the buildings on the opposite side of the street were not there.

'When d'you want to leave?' she said.

'We'll have lunch first.'

'I've been thinking . . .'

'Oh?' He didn't like her thinking. 'What?'

'About what happens afterwards.'

'We take off.'

'Yes, I know. But where to?'

'I thought we'd agreed. Africa. Kenya first, while we look around. Then maybe Durban.'

'Why Africa?'

'I thought you liked the idea.'

'To hell with Africa.'

'And we'd be difficult to find.'

She sat on the bed and stared at him. 'Why do we have to steal the stuff from people like Willi? Why not go to the right places and do business for ourselves? We don't need to deal with middlemen. And I think we should cut Willi in on a deal, not the first one perhaps, but later. It'll make up for this. We don't want enemies everywhere. What's the point of having a great life-style if people are jumping out of the bushes with guns all the time?'

'We'll see,' he said slowly. 'First things first. Let's get the exchange over.'

'And talking about the exchange, sweetie, that needs a bit of a rethink.'

'How d'you mean?'

'Well, correct me if I'm wrong, but the idea was that you stayed in Menton while I crossed into Italy and did the deal in Ventimiglia. Right?'

'Right.'

'Well, I'm not going by myself.'

'But for Christ's sake, why take chances? I'm known in Italy.'

'You've never been arrested there.'

'There's always a first time. Then the whole thing's screwed. Anyway, that was the plan. That's what we agreed.'

'Lady's prerogative. I'm changing my mind.' She

117

flicked his naked chest with her fingernail. 'We do everything together from now on, my darling. Till death us do part, as the man said. Why don't we get some sleep?'

He lay back, but it took him a long time to sleep.

Drac was confused. Things were happening too quickly. He had not planned for that. He needed time. In gaol he had had so much time he had been able to think things out to the last and minutest detail. But here he was being rushed.

He was standing near the fence between the two properties. He had seen the woman come out of the house and walk to the corner. She had looked towards the lime tree. He had ducked. But had he been fast enough? And who was she?

The way she had walked and looked about her had seemed to him to show a familiarity with the place. She wasn't looking around as though to absorb something new, rather as though she was re-familiarising herself with something old.

He went back to his cottage. He found himself hurrying and made himself slow down. Hurry. Rush. He must stop that. But he knew his heart was beating faster than usual. It was because he was being rushed. He had to make decisions. It wasn't a game any longer. He wasn't in the Baumettes planning what he would do. *She was here.* Or at least one of them was.

He could hear the dog jerking at its chain as he went past but hardly gave it a glance. He hurried inside, poured himself a good measure of cognac and threw it down his throat. After a few moments he felt more relaxed, poured a second and sipped it.

If the woman was one of them, which one? He hadn't had more than a quick glance and of course she'd been a girl then.

From the inside of his good 1960s' jacket he pulled out a wallet and from it he extracted a single page torn from an English magazine. He had looked at it so many times that if the power of sight could damage, this page would have been obliterated years ago.

He had once shared a cell with a *rosbif* who was serving time for drug smuggling. The magazine had been his and just this one page had cost Drac dear in cigarettes.

What he saw as he looked at it now was a wedding photograph. The bride and groom were emerging from a register office in London. The caption read: 'Wedding Bells for one of Britain's top models. Flora Fleming weds film cameraman Lou Bryant in Camden Town this week...' The rest of the caption was worn away.

Drac could not read English but he knew every word of the caption for he had had it translated and had memorised it.

He looked more closely. She was turning towards the man, smiling. She was thin and dark and seemed quite tall, taller than the woman he had seen this morning. And her colouring was different.

Which meant he had seen the younger of the two sisters. He had always thought in terms of the other one. But what if she no longer came to the house? She might be living on the other side of the world for all he knew. She might even be dead. Take what you can while you can, he told himself.

But he wasn't ready. It was all too rushed. Suddenly he longed for the timelessness of prison, for the solitude of his bunk. He wanted to do what he had done all those years: he wanted to lie back, put his arms behind his head and think and plan. Those were the moments he had enjoyed.

* * *

119

Dubois made a cup of strong coffee and carried it into the bedroom. Josephine was sitting up in bed with Toutou nestling on her lap. The dog snarled as Dubois lifted it and placed it on its cushion.

'Coffee, my love.'

Josephine hated him to see her without make-up. When he got out of bed to make the coffee she went into the bathroom and came out with her bright blonde hair tied in its ribbon and her lips and cheeks made up.

'Say good morning to papa,' she said to the dog, as she leaned her cheek towards him for the morning kiss. He fetched a cup for himself and sat on the edge of the bed.

She looked good in bed, he thought. And so she should. It was her territory, was it not? She wore an expensive nightdress she had bought in St Tropez, through which he could see her heavy, reassuring bosom.

He lifted one breast as though weighing it and then leaned forward and kissed it.

'Thank you, *chéri*. You want to come back into bed?'

'Better not. I'll be late.'

'We don't want papa to be late. We want him to do something about the house.'

'That's in my mind. I'll give it a good look over. Have something to offer. I mean, the place will rot if it just stands there.'

Josephine scooped up Toutou and placed him against her neck. 'Which house does papa mean? Drac's or the Englishman's?'

'Both, I suppose. It's going to take some money, you know.'

'That's what banks are for. What can Drac want for a ruin?'

'Not much when I've finished with him.' He dressed and drove the five kilometres to Cogolin. As he entered the station the duty officer nodded towards an inner door. 'The Chief wants you.'

120

'What for?'

The officer raised his shoulders slightly.

The Chief was a squat, red-faced man with more than a passing likeness to James Cagney. Sometimes he seemed to trade on it. He often wore bow-ties and his speech was staccato.

'You drink coffee, Dubois?'

'Certainly.'

'Taste that!' He pointed to a tray on his desk.

Dubois was about to say he had had his breakfast but there was a look on the Chief's face that brooked no denial.

'Well?'

'I dunno, it's—'

'It's filthy! It's weak and lukewarm and it's probably decaffeinated. Do you drink decaffeinated coffee, Dubois?'

'No, sir.'

The Chief looked relieved. 'I want you to find out who makes this coffee. Where it comes from. What it consists of. And then report to me. Understand?'

'Yes, Chief. Is that all?'

'No, of course it isn't. You think I'd call you in just for that? Sit down. First of all, Drac. You've seen him?'

Dubois gave a brief description of their meeting.

'What do you think?'

'I dunno. He's not as I thought. After twenty years most of them are a bit gaga. Institutionalised. Can't make decisions. That sort of thing.'

'But not Drac?'

'He seemed to have some confidence.'

'It's a bloody act. He can't have any. They never do. You watch him, Dubois. I want to know every move. Every time he goes for a piss I want you looking over his shoulder.'

'That's what I told him.'

'Make his life a misery. Get him out of here. I don't want him on my patch.'

'I feel the same, sir.'

'I want you to make the Route du Canadel your second home. I want you up there every day. Let him see the car. Let him see you. Understand?'

'Absolutely, sir.'

'And there's something else.'

'Sir?'

'Lebrun had a call from one of his people. He owns a joint the other side of Frèjus, near the autoroute. He's Algerian or Moroccan. He says two men stopped there last night driving a Saab with British plates. Didn't recognise either, but he says they were gypsies. Says the car had a dent in the side and on the roof. But otherwise it looked new. Your gypsies?'

'Maybe.'

'Where are they camped'

'Near La Garde Freinet.'

'Gypsies don't drive around in foreign cars with British plates.'

'Where were they heading, sir?'

'He couldn't be sure. Thinks it's Nice.'

'There's a body shop there that does a good business. Panel-beating. Respray jobs. Cosmetic changes. And then they flog them in Belgium or Holland, maybe even Denmark. It's worth the trouble.'

'All right, tell it to Lebrun. And Dubois . . . the coffee. Don't forget that.'

'Coffee beans,' Roger said. 'Where's the mill?'

They searched the kitchen but there was no grinder.

'In a French kitchen?' he said, with disbelief. He was feeling better. The walk had done him good.

'It's not French it's English,' Jo said. 'Flora probably

sold it. She's got a thing about coffee grinders. Likes to collect them, and sell them. So's Mike.'

She took down a packet of Earl Grey and made tea. Roger cut up the bread. They sat at the big old-fashioned kitchen table. He swallowed a mouthful of tea and looked at her in alarm.

'It's foul, isn't it?' she said. 'Probably been here six months.'

'Is that when you were last here?'

'God, no, I haven't been here for years and years. I told you that. It's Flora who comes.'

'When were you last here?'

'When I was a kid.'

He was looking at her closely. Then he frowned. 'Are you sure?'

'Of course I'm sure. Why shouldn't I be sure?'

'I don't know, it seems odd.'

'If you want coffee there's probably a mill in the van. There're usually one or two in the junk in the back.'

'It doesn't matter.'

He told her he had reported the missing car, but without involving her. He said he had told the police he had skidded off the road and overturned.

'You'll have to put up with me for the rest of the day,' he said. 'The police want me somewhere they can get hold of me.'

She was glad he was staying. Now that she had decided she was not going to go ahead with Mike's plan and had already imagined the dialogue in which she talked him out of the whole thing, she felt better, more confident. And so far she could not fault Roger's story. Their meeting was no more than coincidence.

'And she comes down regularly?' Roger was saying.

'At least once a year, maybe twice.'

'By herself?'

'I suppose so. I've never asked.'

'You're not inquisitive about people, are you? I mean, you take them on trust.'

'You can't go around looking for motives, delving into other peoples' lives.'

'Some people do.'

'Do they?'

'Do you think Flora does? Or Mike?'

'No, of course not. Why?'

'It's just that I don't want them delving into us when we start our affair.'

She laughed. 'You're still on that!'

He smiled with her. 'I like to make you laugh.'

She turned away hastily and began to tidy up.

'What are you going to do?' she said.

'Wait for the police. And you?'

'Wait for Mike.'

She went back to the big armchair and drew the blanket over her again. The house had not warmed up much.

'Biography time,' she said. 'You told me a little about yourself in the restaurant. Start earlier.'

'There's nothing much to tell,' he said. But he began to describe his childhood in New York. He had been speaking for less than a minute when she fell asleep.

16

Willi Trott was annoyed. He was also tired and cold and hungry as he stood outside the car hire firm in Boulogne waiting for it to open. When he was young he had been able to withstand severe cold, long hours and the harassment of his *lingos* stand. But he liked to think those years were over.

He stared in at the empty office. The French were a decadent race. He'd always said so. Effete, soft, arrogant and patronising. Ten past nine and the office was still closed. Didn't they want to do business?

He had phoned his wife Marta from the quayside. She told him that his daughter had done well in her French test the day before. He'd been pleased. Now he rather wished she had done badly. It would teach the French a lesson.

Then Marta had wanted to know when he was getting home and he said he wasn't sure. She said he must have forgotten that it was the family skiing weekend in Semmering. And he'd promised to play tennis on Friday with their son Jerzy. And . . .

For God's sake, he'd said, here he was standing on the freezing quay of a smelly French port and his wife was nagging him from six hundred miles away.

The thing was, Willi thought as he paced the pavement and watched the sea urchins and the oysters and the Atlantic prawns being put out in front of the fishmongers opposite, the thing was that he mustn't be irritated or become out of sorts. That wouldn't solve anything. He had a long drive ahead of him and then a confrontation – if that was how one liked to phrase it – at the end of the road.

Basically Willi liked things to be peacable. Those days of fighting in the Volksprater were long over. And you didn't want to be rough-housing when you were secretary of the tennis club. Kleist didn't. Nobody did any longer. There were other people for that. But there were times when a show of strength was necessary. Lessons needed to be learned.

A raunchy young woman with long legs and tired eyes opened the door of the office.

'I'm sorry,' she said, smiling at him. 'Have you been waiting long?'

'No,' Willi said in his broken French. 'I just arrive.'

Jo woke suddenly, coming out of deep layers of sleep like a dolphin breaking the surface of the water. One second she had been dreaming of the old squat in Battersea, the next she was wide awake. And she was alone.

Was it all imagination? Had Roger ever been there? She curled up tighter. The dream had made her uneasy. There had been someone in the squat with her. She hadn't been able to make him out clearly but had heard him behind her making a kind of hollow knocking noise. She turned to see who it was but there had only been a shadow.

Her mouth tasted awful. She wished she'd never started smoking again.

She heard a noise. It was the one from her dream, a hollow knocking so faint she might have missed it. Was it pipes? Plumbing? No, it didn't sound like that. The mistral had risen and was blowing fiercely. Leaves and sand had come in under the door. Could it be the wind? But it was irregular. And it wasn't the sound of banging as in a branch against the house, or a door or a window. It was too soft for that.

I'm scared, she thought. I'm scared because I'm tired and because I'm doing something I would never normally do in a million years. And I'm scared of this house. I've always been scared of it, come to that.

She heard footsteps upstairs. Her skin crawled. She heard them move down the stone steps. Roger came into the room.

'Feel better?' he said.

'A little. I heard a noise from upstairs. A kind of knocking.'

He nodded. 'So did I. That's what I went to check. I thought maybe a window was open.'

'And was it?'

'No. I think it is water in the pipes. Some old plumbing sounds like that.' He touched her hand. 'You're freezing.'

'It's the room.'

'No. It's warmer now. It's something else. It's being here. The house. Isn't it?'

'Why do you say that?'

'The impression you give.'

'I suppose so. I've always been frightened of it.'

Little Miss Muffet, sat on a tuffet . . .

She forced the memory out of her mind.

'But why?' he said. 'It's only a house. I mean houses do not have feelings or life.'

'Yes they do.'

'It is only people who *think* they do.'

She shivered. The afternoon was beginning to draw in. 'Don't you think that memories remain? A sort of aura? A kind of ectoplasm?'

'You mean in the air of the rooms? In the walls?'

127

'Yes.'

'No, I don't.'

'But it's well known that evil has a kind of existence of its own.'

'Well known to whom?'

'If something terrible happened in a place, something bad, don't you think it might leave a kind of presence, a permanent stain on the atmosphere?'

'No.'

'You're very matter of fact.'

'Do *you*?' He emphasised the word.

'I don't know. I don't like to talk about things like that.'

'Something happened here, didn't it?'

'Why do you say that?'

'All this talk of evil.'

Little Miss Muffet . . .

'I don't know!'

'Yes you do,' he said remorselessly.

'I've forgotten! I don't want to talk about it!'

'He's an evil man,' her grandmother had said, 'and evil men must be punished.'

'The big spider,' Flora had said. 'He'll come and sit down beside you.'

'No!'

'Yes, he will!'

'Just tell the truth,' her grandmother had said.

What was the truth? All these years of trying not to think. 'You're not very inquisitive,' Roger had said. But what if you found out something terrible, worse than you knew? And that was the point: what *did* she know? It was all hazy. It was a long time ago. She no longer knew if her memories were her own or the statements of others.

128

'You want to talk about it, don't you?' Roger said softly. It was like hypnosis. 'Yes,' she said.

She'd never spoken of it except to her grandmother when the police were there. She'd never told Mike the truth, just that her father had died. Nor had Flora. It was an unspoken pact between them.

But maybe it would be all right with a stranger. For Roger was that. A sympathetic stranger who would be leaving soon. If she told him it might clear it from her subconscious. And then there might not be any more sudden flashes, pictures, words – to come crashing into her thoughts.

'Tell me about your parents. Can you remember them?'

'It's like everything else. I can remember some things, others I assume, and still others were told me by my grandmother. It's difficult to separate them.' It had been a difficult marriage. Her grandmother had the wedding photographs and she remembered them quite clearly for she had often looked at them. Her father had been of medium height with thinning hair even then. He had a good-looking broad face with widely-spaced eyes but his lips were too full which gave him a rather decadent look.

Her mother was soft and gentle-looking, almost pre-Raphaelite with a weak, self-pitying mouth.

'He was a bastard!' her grandmother had said. 'Even on the honeymoon he was . . . well, I won't say unfaithful . . . but he was committing adultery in his mind.'

There had been a succession of women in England before they had left to live in France. That had been in the 1950s when he had had a hit in the West End and taken his wife and Flora, then a baby, to France to escape taxes.

First of all they had rented a house then bought some land from Drac's father near La Motte and built a Provençal-style 'farmhouse'.

This was planned to be a holiday home for at that time everything pointed to Fleming being a successful and wealthy playwright.

They had only meant to stay away the statutory tax year but the next play had been a flop and so had the one after that. They had had to remain where they were. Jo's mother, who had always wanted a cosy suburban villa in Dorking or Reigate, had hated France. She had not been able to speak the language and had never made the effort to learn it.

After a while she had begun to drink.

'The poor creature,' Jo's grandmother had said. 'You can't blame her, not when married to him and stuck away in that lonely place.'

Her father continued his affairs, now mostly with women on holiday he picked up in St Tropez.

He then had one or two hits and his wife waited for them to move back to Surrey. But the move never came. He liked it in the sunshine. He decided he would make France their permanent home. When Jo was born her mother was trapped.

'It is not an uncommon story,' Roger said, bleakly. 'Tell me about what happened here.'

Little . . .

She began slowly and haltingly, as though stumbling through a ploughed field, looking for a path. The picture in her mind was vivid though. She saw the road, dusty in the heat, the grapes on the vines, the sun causing heat shimmer.

They were coming back from school along the dusty road. She and Flora. She was too young for a proper school, like the one Flora was at in the village. But she went to a 'pretend' school.

She remembered it only vaguely. It was really a kind

130

of day-centre for pre-school kids run by a woman in the village, where they played with blocks and raffia. Flora would come to fetch her and they would walk home.

She saw the two of them going through the big iron gates. They were carrying little suitcases with their books and crayons. Did she really remember that? Wasn't there a photograph of the two of them setting off to school taken by their father? Wasn't that what she was remembering? The picture not the reality?

'When did you last see the photo?' Roger said.

'Years ago. Flora has it somewhere. You see what I mean about memory?'

'Go on.'

'Well, we came up to the house. We were early for some reason. At least an hour early.'

'You were too small to know that.'

'My grandmother or Flora must have told me. It was a half-holiday, I think.'

'And then?'

'We walked past the swimming pool. And there was something . . . an animal . . . a movement . . . on the terrace . . . ' She stopped and took a deep breath. 'I mean, I thought it was an animal. Then I saw it was two people. My father and the woman from next door. Yvette. I thought they were wrestling. Playing.'

Flora had turned away and gripped Jo by the arm. Her face was knotted with anger. Jo remembered that for she had always been afraid when Flora was angry. She remembered the pain of Flora's grip. She had wanted to cry out but Flora whispered that she must not make a sound. *Not a sound!*

'They were making love, of course.'

'Did they see you?'

'No. We went upstairs and Flora stood by the window and said, "Look, the big spider." She was pointing at the lime tree. It was the woman's husband. I hated him. We both did. He used to come over the wall and walk through the garden and sometimes he would shoot little birds in our trees. Once he shot a hare near the swimming pool. He was horrible.'

'Even in summer? I mean, that's not the shooting season.'

'He never seemed to care. He was only doing it to annoy father. Anyway, Flora said she would watch him from father's study. A little while later he shot them both – father and his wife. I went downstairs but Flora said I mustn't look. That something bad had happened to father.'

'And did you look?'

This was the part she had always tried to keep out of her thoughts. 'Yes. My father had fallen into the swimming pool.'

'You remember that? I mean, you can visualise it still?'

'Oh yes, it's the one thing I'm certain about. I just saw his back and head. He was hanging in the water like one of those free-fall parachutists. What I remember most was the colour of the water. It was a kind of mauve.'

'What happened then?'

'That's all hazy. I suppose the police must have arrested the man. And my grandmother flew to France and the police questioned us here and then again in England.'

'But what could you have told them?'

'Not much. Flora was the main witness.'

'And then he was tried and sentenced?'

'My grandmother used to talk about that. She thought it scandalous he only got five years. But I don't think she was sorry my father was dead. She'd never forgiven him for what he had done to my mother.'

'You said your mother drowned.'

'A year before my father was killed.'

'Do you think...? I mean from what you've told me...'

'Suicide? Yes, I've often wondered. No one will ever know.'

She felt drained. Exhausted. Where she should have found peace she found only depression.

'What happened to the man next door when they released him?'

'They didn't. He killed a guard and got life. He's still in gaol – or dead.'

There was a knock at the door.

Dubois stood in the small pine grove and watched Drac. He was outside the cottage feeding the dog on scraps.

Dubois had left his car some distance down the road and come on foot. He had come quietly but even so had hardly expected to get as close as this without Drac seeing or hearing him. The afternoon had turned dark and cloudy and the mistral was icy.

He made a sound deliberately and saw Drac's head jerk up. That'll teach you, he thought.

As he came to the house Dubois saw the almost empty bottle of cognac on a window-sill; he also saw that in spite of the cold Drac was sweating. The dog growled.

'You still here?' he said to Drac, walking slowly to the door of the house.

Drac did not reply but gave the remainder of the food to the dog.

'He's an ugly brute.'

Drac scratched the dog behind its ear as it wolfed down the food.

Dubois noticed the unsteadiness of his hands, the slight lurch as he got to his feet. Excellent, he thought. Maybe the Chief was right; maybe Drac had been pretending to a confidence he did not have and now was leaning on the old familiar crutch – alcohol. He went into the big kitchen/living-room. Drac followed. 'Well, it's better than it was,' Dubois said. 'But it's still not much.'

He looked around with some attention. The walls were solid, the window frames seemed sound. The flue worked, there was no sign of damp.

'It's worth a bit. Not much, but a bit. You should think of selling up. Get a bit of money in the bank. Buy a small flat where people don't know you.'

'I'm not selling.' Drac said. 'I'm staying.'

'Think about it. I'm going to make your life a misery. You'd be better off somewhere else.'

He climbed the stairs. Drac followed. He poked his head into the two unused bedrooms. The wall-paper was torn and there were patches where rain had come in through broken windows. But what could you expect?

He looked into Drac's room. 'What d'you want a double bed for?' he said. 'Who do you think would come up here? Not even an old tart from Toulon.'

'You've no right to come here,' Drac said.

Dubois smiled to himself. Truculent. All ex-cons were truculent. That was different from the last time too. Then he had been cool, unflappable, dangerous. He turned and looked at Drac, seeing the eyes swimming with alcohol but also seeing something else: confusion? uncertainty? 'Rights? What bloody rights are these? You've got no rights, Drac. No rights at all.' He sniffed. 'You're dirty, I can smell it.'

The big man was bathed in sweat. He was like some bewildered animal, Dubois thought. That was always the problem with lifers. Once they left the cell they were finished.

He went downstairs again. 'You seen any gypsies in a foreign car?'

'No.'

'You bought the dog from one, you told me.'

'They were walking.'

'I'll check. I'll check everthing.'

He finished his evaluation of the house. It would be a good prospect. He would be able to describe it in detail to Josephine.

'You know anything about a stolen car? A grey Saab?'

Drac shook his head.

'Maybe you do, maybe you don't . . . Just remember Drac, I've got my eye on you. Every move you make I'll be watching.'

He went down through the pines towards the road but instead of going to his car he swung round in a circle, entered the pines again and walked up along the wall that joined the two properties. He could now see Drac from a different angle. He was still looking down into the trees in the direction Dubois had taken.

There was a large stone near the wall and Dubois stood on it to look over. Nice house. Better than some of the new villas. More character.

He saw the rear of the VW microbus. So, someone was there. And in winter too. That was unusual.

And then a thought blossomed in his mind. Why not think big? If he bought this place he'd really have something. And he would lay a bet there would not be too much to do in the way of refurbishing. Not like Drac's. He saw himself the owner of not one house but two. Money? The banks – as Josephine had said.

He walked to the big iron gate. He had made up his mind to go in. Just to see what was what. He wouldn't open his mouth about his idea: but it would be good to know who was there.

And if he felt there would be no chance of them selling, there was the other idea; getting the house on his books like the villas.

What if the *rosbifs* learned that Drac was back? Would that help? They might sell for peanuts just to get away.

But you couldn't tell with *rosbifs*. He'd discuss this aspect first with Josephine.

No. Just show the flag. I'm your friendly neighbourhood cop. Anything troubling you, just let me know. That sort of thing.

He knocked at the door.

17

Flora leaned back against the headrest and watched the darkening countryside rush past. Mike was driving at just on a hundred, sweeping everything out of the fast lane.

'Where are we going to eat?' she said. 'I'm hungry.'

They were on the autoroute east of Aix. 'Look up St Maximin in the *Michelin*,' Mike said. 'There may be something there.'

'What are we going to do when we get to La Motte?'

'We've already discussed that.'

'*We* didn't discuss anything. You told me. I don't like the idea of spending the night there. You'd have to sleep with Jo or it would look funny.'

'I've spent a lot of nights with Jo.'

'That was different.'

'We do what we said we'd do. Spend the night. Leave the following morning. Are you worried about Jo?'

'Worried! Good God, no. There'll always be someone to look after Jo. People have been looking after her since day one. My father spoiled her, so did my grandmother. Even now people spoil her. You'd think she was seventeen not twenty-seven. She's always been able to give the impression of being an innocent child.'

'Isn't she?'

Flora paused, looking out of the window. The truck traffic was heavy.

'Innocent? When she was about fourteen she was all

over one of my boyfriends. He was nearly thirty. You
call that innocent? Anyway she's your wife, what do you
think?'

'What do you care?'

'She's my sister.'

He turned to her. 'You don't give a damn about
Jo, you never have.'

'I suppose you do.'

'I did . . . in the beginning. She'll be all right. She'll
go back to London and— '

'Look out!'

A truck had, without warning, pulled into the fast
lane to overtake. The car was almost on top of it. Mike
wrenched the wheel to the right, cut into the slow lane,
found another truck ahead of him, put the car into a long
slide, fought the wheel, found a gap and shot through.

'Jesus!' he said.

Flora was ashen-faced.

A petrol station loomed and Mike pulled in. 'I need
a drink,' he said.

He went into the café and came back with an Orangina,
poured in a good measure of vodka. 'Would you like
one?'

'No, thanks.'

He finished the drink while he was filling up with
petrol. When he came back from paying Flora was sitting
in the driving seat.

'Let's not have an argument,' she said.

'Christ, it wasn't my fault. You saw what that bastard
in the truck did!'

'You were talking. Looking at me. Just do me a favour,
sweetie, stop trying to be Rambo.'

Drac held the bottle of cognac up against the sky. It
was empty. He threw it as far as he could, hearing it
smash against a rock.

'That's it,' he said to the dog. 'Finished.'

He had now drunk nearly a full bottle of brandy and was, for the first time since he had seen the young woman in the garden of the *rosbif*'s house, feeling confident and powerful.

'Wine finished, cognac finished,' he said to the dog, sitting down beside it and stroking its ears. At first the animal jerked away, as though fearing the hand, but then allowed itself to be petted.

'I told you we'd become friends,' Drac said. 'We're all we've got.'

He knew he had to make plans and yet his mind, which seemed crystal clear, refused to function. He had made so few decisions in prison, where everything had been decided for him, that it was as though this part of his mind was rusty. But the brandy helped.

'I'm going to tell her first,' he said. 'She must know why. I want her to know and to be afraid. I was afraid. I didn't show them but I was. You wonder what's going to happen. You wonder if you're ever going to make it. Twenty years. That's a long time. There are not many who can serve twenty years without going mad. But maybe I had enough practice.'

He thought of the years when he had lived in the Forêt des Maures. His father had been away a lot, first driving a truck, then in the army. Those times had been the best, but when his father came back he and his mother had suffered. His father had been a man of aimless violence beating either Drac or his mother whenever he was drunk, which was often.

The memory caused Drac to reach for the bottle and then remembered he didn't have it any longer. He'd have to do something about that. He went into the house and began to clean the shotgun. He looked through both barrels against a candle. They shone with gun oil.

Then he sorted through the cartridges he had taken

from the gypsy. Number fives. Light. But not at close range. At two metres, before the shot had time to spread, they would blow holes the size of dum-dum bullets.

'Not yet,' he said to the dog through the open doorway. 'I won't go yet. I'll wait till full dark.'

And then he sudddenly thought: what do I do when it's over? It almost took his breath away. He had never considered that aspect.

His mind had been obsessed with ritual: cleaning the gun, putting in the cartridges, entering the house, watching the expression on her face (their faces?) as he spoke. It had given him an almost sexual pleasure. And then . . . the shots. They echoed in his head down the years. And the bodies and the blood.

But what about Dubois? He'd come for him for sure. Who else were they going to arrest?

He tried to get his mind to concentrate on this new problem. He could feel the sweat break out again on his face. Then he had it! The gypsies. They'd been around here. Dubois knew that. He knew they all had shotguns. He knew they sometimes robbed houses.

That's what he would do! Make it seem like a robbery. Later he could plant the stuff up in the camp near La Garde Freinet. He wouldn't keep anything. Not even the gun. There would be nothing to connect him at all.

Dubois might wonder. Let him. Maybe he would even sell the house when it was over. Dubois's suggestion was not all that bad.

And then what?

'We'll buy ourselves a cottage deep in the Massif des Maures,' he said to the dog. 'Far from the road, where no one ever comes. Just the two of us.'

His fuddled mind went backwards and forwards over this plan. It was foolproof. But to make it work he needed another drink.

★ ★ ★

140

Dubois pointed to the black speckling of mould in a corner of the living-room and said to Jo, 'It comes from condensation, Madame. In winter the stone floors become cold, but on sunny days the air warms up. Moulds form. What you need is someone who can come in and deal with this.' He walked into the kitchen, looked at the patch of damp under the sink which was pulling off the plaster. Jo and Roger bent to look with him.

'I would have had that done for you. It is part of my service. I have had central heating put into the Lindemanns' villa. I had the top windows replaced in Madame Rival's. I write to them, you know, saying this and that needs doing and they ask me to arrange it.'

They went back to the sitting-room. 'Apart from these matters there is the one of security.' He looked at her gravely. 'I spoke to your sister about this a few years ago. She said she would consider the matter. I have to tell you, Madame, that things have not got better. On the contrary we have more burglaries than ever. So I have time switches that bring on lights. I make my rounds at unexpected hours. It would be like having your own security guard plus concierge.'

'I'll think about it,' Jo said.

Dubois had ignored Roger once he knew he was not Jo's husband. One didn't want to waste one's time with boyfriends.

'And should Madame and her sister ever wish to sell the property I would be pleased to offer for it.' He fumbled in his pocket and gave Jo a business card. 'It is my private address. I would not wish Madame to contact me through the police. This is a personal service, you understand.'

'Perfectly,' Jo said.

'Well . . .'

'I'll think about it,' Jo repeated. 'My sister is coming. We will talk.'

Dubois bowed and Roger opened the door. The outside light was powerful and they watched him walk down the drive and close the gates behind him. It was dark now.

Roger closed the door and stood with his back to it. Jo was standing in the centre of the room. They stared at each other for a long moment and then Jo said, 'Why didn't you mention your car?'

'He's a country cop. What would he know?'

'He's the local cop, of course he'd know.'

She waited for him to reply but he remained silent. There was something terrifying about that silence. It was as though he could not be bothered to lie any more. She moved towards the door but he moved too, covering the handle with his body.

'Will you let me out please.'

'Where are you going?'

'I want to get something from the VW.'

'I'll get it.'

She paused. She was frightened. 'This is my house. I must ask you to leave.'

'I told you, I have to stay. The police will contact me here.'

There was an obvious reply to that but she did not want to provoke him.

'Well, let me out then.'

'I'm afraid I cannot do that.'

'Why not?'

'There are reasons.'

Suddenly she turned and ran to the back door. It was chained and bolted. He reached her easily. She fought him, beating at his head. He stumbled back, surprised at her strength and fell over a chair. She ran to the front door but the key was not in the lock. As he was getting to his feet she ran for the stairs that led to the bedroom with the toy cupboard.

'Joanna,' he called, stretching out to try to stop her,

but she swerved round and took the stairs three at a time. She ran to the room and flung back the door to close it but he was already there. His foot stopped it. He pushed it open and came in slowly.

'Get away from me!'

'I don't mean you any harm. I promise you.'

Her fear was overlaid by anger. She turned on him. 'Dubois is the local police. Of course he'd know! You didn't want to talk about it! You didn't want him to know. Why? I'll tell you, because you never reported the theft. You never reported the accident either! Why are you here? What do you want? *Who are you?*'

'Who are *you?*' Roger said. 'That is the important question. I thought I knew who you were. But now I'm not sure.'

'You conned me and tricked me. You've been following me. You followed me in London. You took pictures of me. And now you've followed me in France. You've been lying to me ever since we met!'

As they came downstairs she thought of the statuette. It was in her bag. And suddenly she knew what to do: let him have it, let him take it and go and then when Mike came she'd tell him what had happened and that would solve everything. The whole plan would evaporate without her having to talk him out of it.

'If you want the statue I'll give it to you!'

'What statue?'

'Oh, for God's sake don't pretend! I don't care about it!' She brought it from her bag. 'Take it! We don't want it! And you can tell that to Willi!'

'Willi?'

For the first time she fought off tears.

He examined the vicuña then put it down on the table. She saw by his face he had no interest in it at all.

He put his arm around her shoulders but she wrenched away. 'Don't touch me!'

'I think we'd better talk,' he said.

'All you've done is talk. You've lied to me from the moment we met.'

'I apologise. If I explain, perhaps you will understand.'

'More lies?'

'Not this time. I swear I will tell you the truth. And then, perhaps you will tell me about the statuette and Willi. You have not been entirely honest with me either.'

'Why should I?'

'Joanna, your life has dominated me for months. Why don't we have a cup of coffee? Shall I look for a mill in the van?'

She suddenly felt drained. 'Do what you want, I don't care.' The one thing she clung to was that Mike would soon be here.

'It's solid,' Dubois said to Josephine. 'Doors, windows and floors are all right. I don't know about the roof.'

They were having an apéritif, this time bought with their own money. Josephine was dressed in a fluorescent gold jump-suit and lay on the black leather sofa with Toutou curled up against her stomach. She had put a large blue ribbon round the dog's neck which trailed on the floor as he walked but which he bore without too much resentment.

'But will he sell?'

'I have a feeling that he might. You know, he was different today. The Chief says none of these twenty-year men have all their marbles. Drac's boozing again. He'll go out tonight. He'll run out of booze or want company. So I'm going to be wherever he is. The moment he puts his foot in the car I'm going to have him.'

'And then?' She addressed this to the dog.

'With all this new fuss about death on the roads and drinking and driving, he's likely to go back for months. And he'll lose his licence.'

'Pressure,' she said.

'That's it, my love.'

He briefly told her about the other house.

'I don't know if they're interested though. I did the security angle.'

'You told them about Drac?'

'No. Not yet. I wanted to discuss it with you first. You have a way of seeing things.'

'Yes,' she said without mock-modesty. 'That's true.'

He rose. 'If my hunch is right he'll start at the bar in La Motte. I better get going.'

'Toutou wants papa to take care.'

'I always do.'

18

Roger came back into the house with a coffee mill in his hand. It was large and ornate, made of mahogany with a pewter bean holder and pewter handle.

'It is very attractive,' he said, holding it up. 'These old ones are heavy.'

Jo did not respond.

'You know there are fifteen or twenty more in the VW?'

'I told you, Mike and Flora like them,' she said dully.

He pulled at the little drawer but it would not move. She watched him with interest. She was enduring now. Waiting for Mike.

She said, 'I don't want coffee. I want something stronger.' She crossed to a cabinet. There was an un-opened bottle of whisky among half a dozen empty vodka bottles. She poured herself a shot and returned to the chair. Roger said, 'May I have one?'

'Help yourself.'

He sat on the sofa facing her. 'You're not going to like what I say,' he began.

'That'll make a change!'

'It means hurting you. I never thought I'd be sorry, but I am. Once I thought that would be the best thing in the world, hurting you and Mike.'

The whisky was making her feel more human. 'I've no idea what you're talking about. It sounds crazy. Why would you want to hurt me?'

'Someone has to make restitution for what happened.'

Suddenly it was the Willi scene all over again. 'Look,' she said. 'You're making a mistake. You've been following the wrong person. So whatever this is about you might as well stop now. I don't want to know. I don't need to know. *I'm the wrong person.*'

His smile matched the bleakness in his eyes.

'But you are the *right* person. You are Joanna Fleming born here in France at the Les Pyramides *clinique* in St Tropez—'

'I told you that!'

'You told me you were born in France, not exactly where. Your mother died from drowning when you were five. And you were wrong, it was not from Pampelonne beach, but further along, on Tahiti beach. And they never found her body. You did not tell me that. Your father died a year later. Killed in what the papers called a "love triangle" here at this house. His murderer's name was Marcel Henri Drac.'

She felt her skin begin to contract.

'Drac was sentenced to five years' imprisonment but then killed a warder and was sentenced to fifteen more. Am I right so far?'

'Yes.' Her voice was no more than a whisper.

'Your father wrote thrillers for the stage. The last one was called *The Spider's Web.*'

There came a big spider, and sat down beside her.

'You see? You *are* the right person! At home in London I have a file full of information about you and your family and Mike. I can even give you the address of your sister's flat in Camden Town.'

'But *why?*' she burst out.

'I'm going to tell you why. But first I must go back a little. I told you about my father and mother and growing up in America. But I did not tell you about Justine.'

'Justine! The name in the letter!'

'So you're not the little innocent after all. You read my letter!'

'You would have done the same. I wanted to believe in you. After I read the letter I did.'

He nodded. 'So you know the name Justine. Let me tell you about her. There are some people who have all the luck in life. Golden people. Clever and beautiful and amusing and trustworthy and caring and . . . You must have come across people like that. You think to yourself: it's not fair.

'These golden people will always get the jobs they want and the marriages they want. They will have the children they want. The house they want. The life they want – all without too much effort. In a way you remind me of Justine.'

'I can tell you you're wrong!'

'Maybe. Anyway, I knew her well. She had a degree in political philosophy from the Sorbonne and could speak four languages fluently; English and French to perfection. She became a freelance simultaneous translator.

'Sometimes she worked at the International Court in The Hague, sometimes at conferences in Geneva, sometimes at the European Parliament in Strasbourg. She had a marvellous life. She was highly paid and she was beautiful and several men were in love with her.'

'Including you.'

'Oh yes, I loved her too, even more deeply than the others. Then a few years ago she came down for a holiday to St Tropez and for the first time in her life *she* fell in love. Really and truly in love.

'It was October. The tourists had gone and St Tropez was settling down for the winter.

'It is the best time to be there. Senequiers is half empty. The waiters actually welcome you. The stall holders in the market are polite, friendly – all very different from the height of summer.

'There is also a . . . *tristesse* in the air of a place like that when the season has come to an end. A sadness, a melancholy. Justine was in tune with such a feeling for deep down she was a true romantic. At least that is what I thought at the time.

'She had come to St Tropez for more than a holiday. It had been to get away from a love affair in Paris which had gone bad.

'The man was not-bad-looking, there was money in the family, he was charming and amusing. Unfortunately he was married. He told Justine that he would get a divorce, but when the time came he backed off because his wife threatened to kill herself.'

'You?'

'No, no, not me. Not yet. Anyway Justine met this man, an Englishman, in St Tropez. He owned a yacht and lived aboard. It was not one of the big fashionable yachts but a good sailing boat.

'Whether it was because the affair in Paris had ended I can't say, but she fell heavily in love with him.

'I think it may have been partly because he wasn't French. Instead of the highly-charged, febrile intellectuals she was used to, this man was of the outdoors. He was *different*. How different she did not, of course, know at the beginning.

'He was big and good-looking and he could sail his yacht single-handed. They met in one of the harbour bars in the way people do meet. I think he saw that her handbag had fallen open beneath her chair and told her. Something like that. It was the start.

'They talked, had a drink together, then lunch. Lingered over coffee. Had a few more drinks. Dinner. He took her sailing. She drove him to Cannes and St Paul and Bandol for long, lazy lunches.

'She had a room in one of the hotels but it was not long before she was spending most of her nights with him in his yacht.

'And now she really fell for him. She wanted to be with him all the time. But he would not tolerate that. Sometimes he would sail out of St Tropez without telling her and be away for a couple of days and she would sit in Senequiers until darkness watching the harbour mouth.

'This had never happend to her before. Men were always falling in love with her, chasing after her, buying her expensive gifts. But he did none of these things. He treated her with indifference. If he wished he went out with her, if he did not then she had to put up with it.

'Once, when he had been away without telling her she screamed at him, telling him he was a thoughtless bastard. He hit her, cutting open her eyebrow with his ring.

'In the middle of the fight he grabbed her and took her there on the floor of the cabin with all the dirty ropes and pieces of canvas around them. She told me nothing like it had ever happened to her before. It was the first time she had ever really known what the sexual act was all about. You want another drink?'

Jo handed him the glass in silence. When he returned with her whisky she said, 'It's fascinating, but what's it got to do with me?'

'I'll come to that. Anyway, Justine became besotted by him. I remember phoning her sometime in November and asking when she was returning to Paris and she said she did not know. That was strange, for she always knew her movements weeks, even months, in advance.

'By December her friends were worried. I was too. I told you I loved her very much. I took a few days leave and drove down to St Tropez. I found a very different Justine.

'She had taken a room overlooking the port. When I

150

got there he had gone for a few days. She never knew where he went or when he was returning. Her window had a view of the harbour mouth and she would sit at it hour after hour watching for him.

'I told you that in Paris she was a beautiful young woman, well dressed, fashionable. She had changed. Her dark hair was pulled back in a pony tail, her clothes were uncared for. She used little make-up and there were dark rings under her eyes.

'I took her out for drinks and, especially, meals because she had lost weight. She would not eat anywhere other than the restaurants or bars which overlooked the port.

'She would sit facing the harbour and when I spoke she seemed to hear only half of what I said. Her eyes always looked over my shoulder. It was unnerving.

'She spoke quite freely about him. She knew what was happening to her and she did not seem to care although deep down I think she did.

'She knew he was not very bright, she knew he was callous and indifferent, yet she wanted only to be with him.

'When he was there life had a different density. Even talking about her real work bored her. To be with him was exciting and their fights usually ended in love-making of an intensity she had thought she would never experience.

'I tried to argue with her, to talk her out of what she was doing. I told her all the reasons she should give him up. She knew them. The more I talked the more distant she became until I finally returned to Paris.'

In spite of herself Jo had been caught by the story. 'You must have loved her very much.'

'Very much. I lost touch with her after that. She had said she would write but didn't. I wrote to her and telephoned half a dozen times then I was told she had left St Tropez and followed him to Antibes.

151

'I went down again and tried to find her. I searched everywhere. Finally I came to a small yacht marina between Juan les Pins and Antibes.

'As usual no one seemed to recognise my description of her but when I said she had been with an Englishman, one of the yachtsmen said there had been a "hippy" woman at the marina several times.

'I asked if there were any other hippies and was told of a small group that hung out at a little rocky beach near the marina.

'I found half a dozen young people smoking marijuana and spoke to them. They were suspicious at first but when I gave them money they told me they knew Justine. She had been with an Englishman until finally he had sailed away one day and never come back.

'She had sat on the beach day and night for nearly two weeks, waiting for him. When he didn't return she too disappeared, some thought in the direction of Cannes. I reported her to the police there as a missing person and then returned to Paris. There was nothing more I could do.'

He fumbled in his pocket, looking for cigarettes. Jo said, 'I'm sorry. Here. They're yours.'

He took one and said, 'Keep them.' She lit his and one for herself and tucked the cigarettes and lighter back into her shirt pocket.

'I was to see Justine only once more,' he went on. 'I was in the office one night about a month later when I received a telephone call from the Cannes police. They told me that she was dead. There was a letter from me among her belongings so they had got in touch with me to come and identify the body.

'I flew down to Cannes. She was in the morgue. I went with a policeman who said to one of the morgue staff, "We've come to look at the throwaway."

'I did not understand him. I was shown her body.

She was naked and so thin I wanted to cry. She was like those pictures you see of the survivors of Dachau or Belsen.

' "Look at the tracks," the cop said. I saw the needle marks on the inside of both arms.

' "She must have been beautiful once," the morgue attendant said.

' "Who cares about throwaway people?" the cop said.

'I was angry. I threatened to report him. He laughed at me. He said the Côte d'Azur was crawling with people like her. She was better off dead and so was society.

'I went back to the little beach and found the group of hippies still there. They remembered me. I told them what had happened to Justine. They did not seem surprised.

'They told me she had been mainlining for months and drinking cheap alcohol. They said it had only been a matter of time before she overdosed.

'It had never occurred to me that she might have been on heroin. I said I could hardly believe that someone like her could have been hooked. I asked them if they used heroin. They said no. Then where did she get it? The Englishman, they said. He had started her on heroin and had continued to supply her.

'The police had given me the address of her room. When you're on the Croisette in Cannes you never think there might be a poor quarter. But back of the main town, near the autoroute there is an area where the Arabs live. It was a dark room in a smelly hovel. There was a mattress on the floor. Her clothes had been stolen but there were still papers and letters lying about. That's how I got the name.'

'What name?'

'The Englishman's, her lover.'

'And?'

'I decided to look for him. A job came up in the

London office and I applied for it. Marie-Claire—'

'You were married?'

'Oh yes. We went to London and I spent every minute of my spare time and a lot of time I should have been working, looking for him, finding out about him.'

'And did you find him?'

'It took some time but the yachting world is not too big. I found out that he had sold the yacht and had gone into business for himself. He had also married. So that meant I had to investigate his wife and her family too.'

He paused.

Jo felt the cigarette burn her knuckles. She was shivering now, not with the cold. 'Stop it! Stop it! It's not true!'

'I'm afraid it is.'

'I don't believe it!'

'Of course you don't, he's your husband. You've known him a lot longer than you've known me. Why *should* you believe me?'

'It's someone else! You've made a terrible mistake. You've blundered into something without any proper background and now you suspect—'

'I even suspected you.'

'Of what, for God's sake?'

'Dealing with drugs.'

'You must be insane.'

'But there are some people who are transparently honest. I think you're one.'

She brushed this aside. 'And you think Mike was her lover?'

'I don't think. I know. She kept a diary, notes, the name of the yacht. That sort of thing.'

'But Mike doesn't own a yacht.'

'He sold it before you met. He was already in antiques then, wasn't he? What did he tell you he'd done after leaving the army?'

'That he'd . . . he'd travelled a lot. He didn't know what he wanted to do. He was just filling in time.'

'He left the army three years ago. And "left" is not quite the word. He was allowed to resign. There was a problem with a woman in Hamburg. When he threw her up she wrote to the army authorities denouncing him as a drug trafficker. Nobody could prove anything but it was thought advisable for him to resign.'

'That's rubbish! I'd know if Mike took drugs.'

'I didn't say he took them, I said he trafficked in them.'

She got up and stood over him. 'I want you out!'

'Listen to me for one minute more.'

'No! I've heard enough! Go away!'

He rose and faced her. 'Are you afraid of the truth?'

'It isn't the truth! It's lies!'

'Last Sunday night after Camden Lock Market closed you drove to your house in Pimlico. A little while later a man came out. Then you went in a hurry to your sister's flat in Camden Town.'

'So?'

'You stayed there for a while, maybe an hour and then your husband came to the door, yes?'

'He came down from Scotland. He phoned from the motorway.'

'What if I tell you your husband telephoned you from a call box just outside your sister's flat?'

'That's nonsense.'

She was desperately trying to remember. 'I was there,' Roger said. 'And he did not come from the motorway, he came from your sister's flat.'

'That's a lie!'

'I saw him. He came out and went to the call box and telephoned you. While he was talking I pretended to use the phone. I opened the door to get a close look at him.'

'I don't believe it!'

Somebody wants to use the bloody phone, Mike had said.

She suddenly changed her tack. 'I know what this is all about. Okay, Mike took your girl. I'll believe that much. And you're eaten up with jealousy. Humiliated. That's why your marriage wouldn't work. You lost Justine *and* your wife. And now you'll do anything to get even.'

'That's not true, Joanna.'

'And you're a journalist. This is the sort of story people like you write every day of the week and if you make up half of it, who cares? I should have spotted that at the very beginning.'

He shook his head slowly. 'No, it's not like that at all. She wasn't my girlfriend, she was my sister.'

'Your sister!'

'My twin sister. We had been very close. We loved each other very much. When I saw her naked body in the morgue I swore I'd find the man who started her on drugs. I *had* to, you see. The police wouldn't have moved. She was a throwaway person, remember.'

'But if it was true maybe it didn't happen as you said. Maybe . . . God you've got me almost believing you!'

'Remember the phone call. He lied about that. People who lie about one thing usually lie about others.'

'If it is true, if . . . well, what are you going to do?'

'Go to the police with the evidence. He's still trafficking. All these trips to Vienna and the Continent and around Britain. Do you think he's just buying and selling antiques? I think he's using this house.'

She stared at him. 'The police!'

'Interpol. They have a drug squad and they cross borders.'

'Oh God! That's why you came here. That's all you wanted, wasn't it? For me to lead you to him.'

'Not to him. I can find him anytime. To the drugs. The system.'

'But there aren't any!'

'I have to look.'

'It was you!'

'What?'

'Tapping on the walls.'

He nodded. 'I'm going to go on searching now.'

'No.'

'Listen, Joanna. I like you. Very much. At first I thought you were mixed up in it too. I now believe you're not. But will the police?'

She could find no reply.

'I've told you all this for your own sake. Now get in the VW and drive to a hotel somewhere. Get away from here.'

'I can't. Don't you see he's my husband! He trusts me. Anyway I've only heard your story. I still don't believe you.'

He shrugged. His face was grim. 'Keep out of my way then and you won't get hurt.'

'It's *my* house!'

'I'm sorry.' He was making for the staircase when they heard a car. As it swung into the drive the headlights briefly lit up the corners of the room.

'Mike!' Jo ran towards the door. As she did so her coat knocked the little vacuña from the table. It fell on to the tiled floor.

'Oh God!' She went down on her knees beside it. It was broken, or at least a part of it had come away. She saw that it was in two parts, an outer covering of baked clay. Part of the clay had broken away in the fall, exposing the inner section. Gold, Mike had said. But it wasn't gold, it was nothing more than lead.

She turned to Roger. She wanted to show him. But the room was empty. She heard the back door close. Then she heard the car doors slam and footsteps came across the gravel towards her.

She was alone.

157

19

Drac stood at one end of the La Corniche bar in La Motte. His eyes were staring down the bar-top making the other drinkers uncomfortable. Several had moved away and were standing in a group near the door with their backs to him.

Julien, the owner, stood in the middle of the bar at the bead-covered archway leading into his accommodation. He was a spare, sallow man, with poor teeth and he was thinking that if Drac became a regular customer he'd go out of business. He couldn't see the locals coming in for a jolly evening with that big, glowering head dominating the bar.

But Drac was not looking at anyone in particular. His eyes were unfocused, he was staring at nothing.

He had a pastis in front of him. It was his third and they were mixing violently with the brandy. His mind was fuzzy and far away, full of the sounds of prison: the keys, the doors, the cries. He could smell the latrine odour which had enveloped the place mingling with the decaying, damp walls.

Why was he thinking of that? Why was he remembering? He did not want to remember yet he could not get the thoughts out of his mind. He had imagined that part of his life over and forgotten, but it haunted him and he fought it.

As a small boy he had suffered from boils. At one time there had been forty in the small of his back. The feeling he had now was of a great boil in his skull that needed lancing. He told himself that once he had done what he had to do he would have relief.

The bar was hot and his face was red and sweaty. His two huge hands, 'weapons' the judge had called them, lay on the bar-top like pieces of butcher's meat.

Another vision came into his mind of the cottage he had lived in with his mother before the war. It had been deep in the Massif where the charcoal burners lived.

That had been the one reasonably happy part of his life. He would go back there and take Bizetta with him. They would look after each other. In the winter he would shoot hares and partridges and he would cook them as he had done as a boy, over a fire of cork oak wood.

He wouldn't have to talk to anyone and no one would talk to him. It was a kind of vision.

But first he had his mission. Nothing good could ever happen until that had been completed. It was a pity only one of the sisters was at the house but he would have to be content with her. There had also been a man. He'd seen him earlier coming back from the village with a baguette. He'd have to go too, of course. There must be no witnesses this time.

Suddenly into his mind flashed the picture of Fleming and Yvette on the terrace. The sweat came out on his face again and he ground his teeth so loudly that drinkers at the far end of the room turned to look at him. He was not aware of them.

Nor was he aware that the telephone in the bar was ringing. Julien answered and in a moment went through the archway.

Jo thought, 'You're an actress – act!'

The door of the house opened and Mike stood there. 'Thank God you're here,' she said. She put her face up to be kissed but he gave her a peck on the cheek.

'Christ it's cold,' he said. 'Bloody mistral.'

Then she saw Flora. She looked out of a magazine: long fawn suede coat over black boots and a white scarf wound round her neck. Her black hair was ruffled from the wind.

Shaken, Jo pulled away from Mike.

Flora said, 'Hi, sweetie. When Mike said he was coming down I thought, what the hell, I'd come for the ride. D'you mind?'

It wasn't really a question. She too kissed Jo on the cheek.

In Jo's hand, behind her back, was the statuette. It seemed to her they must instantly wonder why she was keeping one hand hidden. But they hardly gave her a glance. As they brought in the cases she put it in the bureau drawer. She would not mention it, wait for him to ask her for it.

Mike brought the cases in and rubbed his hands. 'I could do with a drink.'

Jo said to Flora, 'I brought these blankets down because I was cold. You'll need them for your bed, I'll help you.'

Flora caught Mike's eye and smiled. It was a slight twisting of the bright red lips. 'We'll work out the sleeping arrangements later, sweetie.'

Mike was rummaging in the liquor cabinet. 'Empty, empty, empty, empty,' he said bringing out the vodka bottles. 'Who've you been entertaining, Jo?' Flora gave a gravelly laugh.

He pulled a bottle of vodka from his suitcase. 'No tonic,' he said. 'Any in the fridge?'

He walked through to the other room as though he knew exactly where everything was yet, as far as Jo knew, he had never been in this house before.

Act.

He came back. '*Nada*. I'll go down to La Corniche and get some in a minute.'

He carried their bags upstairs. She heard him go into

the big bedroom, the one her father and mother had used, the one with the double bed.

'How were the roads?' she said, when he came down.

'Marvellous. Much better than the British motorways. We hardly saw a thing, did we?'

Flora did not reply, she was looking at Jo.

How had Flora known they were coming to France, Jo thought? How had Mike been able to tell her if he had gone straight off to Wales? Anyway Flora was supposed not to be at home. That's what he had said.

'Not like last Sunday,' Jo said.

'What?' He was fumbling in his pocket for cigarettes.

'You know, when you were coming down from Scotland. You phoned me. Told me the traffic was hell.'

He did not bother to reply.

'Where was it?'

'Where was what?'

He was still roaming about the room as though he might discover tonic water hidden behind the curtains or on the mantelpiece.

'Where you phoned from.'

'What difference does that make?'

'I just wondered.'

'Some service place. I never know the names.'

'I could hear the traffic,' she said.

'Someone opened the phone booth door. Wanted to use the phone.'

Jo was feeling sick. Her hands felt clammy.

'Anyone got a light?'

She passed him Roger's lighter. He lit up and looked at it.

'Where did you get this?'

'I bought it. I bought cigarettes too. I was – bored waiting.'

'I'll fetch the tonic now.' He went out and a gust of freezing air blew across the floor.

161

'Have you put the central heating on?' Flora said.

'I don't know how to.'

'I don't know how to,' Flora mimicked her in a small girlish voice.

She went into the room next to the kitchen and switched on the boiler.

Act.

Jo followed her and said, 'Are you going to wait for a drink or would you like some coffee?'

'You sound like you're playing Her Ladyship in one of father's plays. So gracious, my dear. But since you ask, both. Coffee now and a drink when Mike gets back.'

They went into the kitchen. Flora leaned against the sink, her right elbow cupped in her left hand, a cigarette held close to her face.

'You've been hitting the bottle, I see,' she said, looking at the two glasses. 'Company?'

'One had fly specks in it. I got another.'

'Well, how do you like it?'

Jo was filling the kettle.

'What?'

'The house. You haven't been here for years.'

'It's all right,' Jo said.

Flora gave the same gravelly laugh. 'Rubbish. I bet you were scared stiff. That's why you got the cigarettes.'

Jo found the packet of coffee beans and looked round for the coffee mill. She went into the sitting-room. It was on the sofa where Roger had placed it and had been covered by one of the blankets.

Flora was standing at the kitchen window straining to look out, her hands cupped on either side of her eyes to block out the light.

'What's the matter?' Jo said, putting down the coffee mill on a work-top.

'I thought I heard something.'

'What?'

162

'You needn't be scared. Flora's here to look after you.'

Jo put the beans in the bean holder and began to turn the handle. It stuck. She thought there might be something in the little drawer that was causing it to stick. She took a long-bladed meat knife and started to prise it open.

'Where did you get that?' Flora said, sharply.

Julien went out into the chilly darkness and looked at the line of cars in the little *parking*. He could see a dark shadow in one and went to it. Dubois was lying back in his seat watching the bar entrance.

'Is he still drinking?' Dubois said.

'Sopping up pastis.'

'Good.'

'You're wanted on the phone. Take it in the house.'

Frowning, Dubois went into Julien's front door and picked up the phone. It was a colleague, Lebrun.

'How the hell did you know I was here?' Dubois said.

'I asked Josephine. It would be easier if you were in radio contact.'

'I'm under the mountains. It never works here.'

'Listen, we went to Nice. Carrosserie Joubert.'

'And?'

'You were right. We roughed him up a little. Told him we'd wire his prick to the battery of a Volvo he had in the yard and then start the engine. That got him talking. He said the two gypsies had tried to sell him the Saab but he didn't want it. It was too badly bent.'

'Where did they go?'

'He doesn't know.'

'You believe him?'

'The car wasn't there.'

'Did he know who they were?'

'Figeras and Espino. You know them?'

'One of them, maybe.'

163

'That's why I contacted you. They may come back your way.'

'I'll watch out. What was the colour?'

'Of what?'

'The Saab!'

'Silver-grey.'

Dubois put down the phone as Julien entered the room.

'He's just gone.' Julien said. 'I couldn't stop him. Left the money and went.'

'Shit! Which way?'

'Cogolin.'

'Okay, I'll find him if I have to look in every bar between here and Ste Maxime.'

20

Watching through the window, Roger saw Jo take the knife and begin to try and open the coffee mill.

Flora ran across the kitchen. 'Stop it!' she shouted. 'Leave it!'

'What's the matter with you?' Jo said.

'I've told you a thousand times. Leave those coffee grinders alone! Give me that knife.'

Jo dropped the knife and ran through to the sitting-room, carrying the coffee mill. Flora came after her, grabbing at her shirt.

Roger moved to another window.

'Give me that or I'll—'

'Or you'll what?' Jo said.

Act.

But the acting was over. She'd had enough. 'You want it! Take it!'

She threw the coffee mill at Flora's head. It missed by a foot but smashed against the wall behind her. It fell to the floor. White powder spilled out on to the Provençal tiles.

'You little bitch!' Flora yelled.

'So it's true! Mike *is* trafficking!'

'It's none of your damn business!'

Flora bent to the spilled heroin and began to scoop it back into a burst plastic bag that had come from the interior of the coffee mill.

Outside, Roger had seen all he needed to. The proof was there. Now the police could act. He turned away and made for the gate. He thought he heard a kind of scraping noise at the wall but it was only the lime tree branches being tossed by the wind. For a moment he thought of taking the VW bus but dismissed it. The other coffee mills were there. This was where the proof was needed, at the house.

The village was about three kilometres away. He reached the road and began to run. Just before he came to the main road he saw a white BMW turn into the Route du Canadel. He threw himself down in the scrub.

Inside the house Jo said, 'You've known all the time! You used me from the start. The vicuña! Pre-Colombian! And all the time you wanted me to bring ... You're his—'

The door burst open and Drac stood on the threshold. He was holding the shotgun at waist-level. His heavy face was red, his eyes angry.

They stared at him. Flora opened her mouth, closed it.

'You know me?' Drac's speech was slurred.

'I—'

'Twenty years ago. Remember?'

'My God!' Flora said. 'You! What d'you want?'

'Justice.'

Flora said, 'You must be mad, coming here after what you did. If I pick up that phone you go back to prison. Do you understand that?'

'Never.'

He came further into the room. Jo moved towards the stairs. He swung the gun around. She stopped. 'Why are you doing this?'

'Ask her,' he indicated Flora with the shotgun barrel. 'You were only a little one. It is unfortunate for you but there is no other way. Where is the man?'

'Not far!' Flora said. 'You'd better clear out before—'

'Good,' Drac said. 'It is only us. The same three.'

The mistral was roaring round the house, dust blowing in the open door. And then, behind Drac, Jo saw Mike. He had a stone the size of his fist in his right hand and brought it down on Drac's head. It made a wet noise, like a fish slapped down on a slab.

He had used all his strength but even so Drac half-turned before he fell. He sprawled face down on the cold floor.

'What the hell's going on?' Mike said.

Flora said, 'He was the one who killed our father.'

Mike bent down and studied Drac's face. 'I think he's finished.'

'My God if you'd been five minutes later!'

'What are we going to do with him?' Mike said.

'Nothing,' Flora said. 'Leave him where he is. Call the police.'

'Are you crazy?'

'Mike—' Jo began.

He ignored her, 'You think we want the police sniffing about now?'

'What do they know about us? Nothing! He threatened to kill us. You defended us. He's a madman. He's been in prison for years. He's already a double murderer.'

'No police!' Mike said.

'What are you going to do?'

'What I said I was going to do.'

'All right. If that's what you want. Jo can stay.'

'I mean alone,' Mike stressed.

'What!'

'That's right. On my tod. Solo.'

Flora's face began to knot in the rage Jo knew so well. 'You bastard!'

Mike said, 'It wouldn't have worked. I don't like taking orders. Specially from you.'

'If you think you're walking out on me you're bloody crazy!'

But it was Flora who seemed crazed to Jo. There was a mad, hysterical look in her eyes.

'Jo's got more right to be angry,' Mike said. He turned to his wife. 'Why don't you say something?'

'Justine,' she said.

He blinked as though she had struck him. 'How did you know?'

Out of the corner of her eye Jo saw Flora pick up Drac's gun.

'Be careful with that!' Mike said.

Then she shot him. The noise in the confined space was tremendous. The force of the blast seemed to pick Mike up and hurl him backwards. His face wore an expression of enormous surprise. His own voice and the noise of the gun were the last sounds he ever heard.

The two women stared at each other. In the numbing silence after the shot they could hear, close by, the baying of a large dog.

'You're insane!' Jo began to run for the door. She sensed, rather than saw the shotgun barrel swing towards her. She swerved to the staircase as the gun went off again.

She ran upstairs. Crashed into a door in the darkness, ricochetted into a room. Half fell on one of the beds. Then she was pulling at the toy cupboard door. She was inside. She shot the bolt. The smell of lavender encompassed her. Soothing her. She was safe.

Willi Trott was angry. He had taken a short-cut from the autoroute – at least it had looked like a short-cut on the map – and had spent nearly fifty minutes caught up in a maze of small roads that took him deeper and deeper into the Massif. Now at last he had found La Motte.

His map, however, did not show the Route du Canadel

168

and Willi was not prepared to take more chances with the French country lanes. He sat in his car near La Corniche working out sentences in his limited French. *'Excusez moi m'sieu. Puede usted . . .'* No, no, that was Spanish.

He was embarrassed about going into La Corniche and asking the direction in front of everyone but there seemed to be no other way. He adjusted his toupee and put on his hat. He was just getting out of his car when he saw a phone booth outside the PTT on the opposite side of the road. A man was using the phone. Willi waited until he replaced the receiver, then went up to him.

'Excusez moi, m'sieu, connaissez-vous la Route du Canadel. Je vais, ah . . . Je vais une maison . . .'

Roger was looking at his hat. The one with the feather in it.

'Sprechen sie Deutsch?' Willi said.

'I can speak English if that's any help.'

'I speak a liddle. I look for Route du Canadel, and house . . .' He consulted a piece of paper. *'Haus* Fleming.'

The hat, the feather, now the house. This was the man he had seen coming out of Jo's house. Could this be Willi?

'I know the Route du Canadel,' Roger said.

He had seen, next to La Corniche, a small road leading away from the village God knew where.

'Take that little road there,' he said pointing. Then take the second left. Then first right. The Route du Canadel is off to the left. About five kilometres.'

'Two times to left,' Willie said. 'One to right and then left.'

'That's it,' Roger said.

'Danke sehr. Zank you.'

'A pleasure.'

He watched Willi get back into the car and drive on to the small winding track that went into the Massif. But what if the road petered out after half a kilometre? What if Willi found the real road? The real house?

He began to run back the way he had come.

Little Miss Muffet ... sat on a tuffet ... eating her curds and whey ...

The voice was soft, almost childlike and seemed not more than a few inches away from Jo. She was sitting in the toy cupboard. There was hardly enough room for her panda and herself so she had dragged it on to her knees. There was a light in the cupboard but Jo did not want it shining through the cracks to give away her presence and so she sat in the dark.

There came a big spider ... and sat down beside her ...

'The big spider's dead, isn't he, Jo?' Flora whispered. 'You remember the big spider, don't you? He killed daddy and the lady, didn't he?' Her voice was sing-song and it shot Jo back through the years to her childhood. 'And now Mike's killed him. Good riddance, don't you think?'

Jo held her breath. Flora was so close it was as though her lips were against Jo's ear.

'I know you're in there, Jo. You have to be. There isn't anywhere else. And it was always your favourite place, wasn't it. Your "house" you used to call it.'

Yes, Jo thought. It had been her 'house'. But then she had been smaller and it had seemed larger.

'Are you frightened, Jo?'

The voice was still a sibilant whisper.

Jo thought: don't answer. Whatever you do don't answer. And then: there's nothing she can do. Maybe I can't get out, but she can't get in. Then she began to think about the shotgun. She'd fired both barrels. But what if the man had more cartridges on him? Did Flora know how to load a shotgun? Of course she did. She'd had boyfriends who shot pheasants and her first husband had gone to Scotland every year for the grouse.

'If I were you, Jo, I'd be frightened.'

In which case why hadn't she reloaded and blown the lock off the door. Because there weren't any more cartridges, that's why.

There was always Roger. She did not know where he was or what he was doing but if he was investigating Mike then he must be somewhere around. In her 'Dear Roger' letter his wife had accused him of being obsessed with the case. If he was obsessed he wouldn't leave. He might even have seen what had happened. If so he would have gone to the police.

So she must hang on. Just keep silent and hang on. Flora couldn't be absolutely one hundred per cent certain that she was in here, for the door also locked from the outside and Jo had the key in her pocket.

The door handle suddenly rattled. 'If you think you're bluffing me you're wrong,' Flora said. Her voice sounded annoyed. Suddenly Jo had a memory of childhood. Sometimes she would come in here to get away from Flora and eventually her sister would become irritated at being ignored and begin to rattle on the door handle – as she was doing now.

'I looked through the other rooms, under the beds, behind the doors. You couldn't have hidden and I doubt you could have got downstairs while I was searching. So you *must* be in here.'

Was there just the slightest hint of doubt?

'Anyway, I think you are and that's what counts. Just you and me as we always were. Me out here and you in there. Remember the time you wouldn't come out and I threw the key away and father had to get a new one made before he could let you out?'

171

Flora had tried to frighten her but had got it wrong. She had *liked* to be in the toy cupboard by herself. That was the whole point. Other children would have screamed and become hysterical, but it was Jo's place, her territory.

'It's all right, my darling,' her father had said when he returned with the new key. 'We'll soon have you out. Don't worry.'

But she hadn't worried. He was the one who had. He'd also been angry with Flora. Jo had never seen him so angry. Later, after her mother died, he had not wanted her to play there any longer. He feared she might suffocate. And so he had changed the lock and it became a store-cupboard, so crammed with bits and pieces that she could not have squeezed in even had she wished to.

There was a long silence. She thought she knew what Flora was doing. She was listening at the wall. But Jo was breathing softly through her mouth and her face was pressed into the panda's ancient fur. It, too, smelled of lavender.

'Hello there!' Flora said. 'I'm back, Miss me?'

Liar! Jo thought.

'Just went to close the shutters. Wouldn't do for anyone to peek inside before I was ready. I'm nearly ready now. It's quite an interesting scenario. Would you like to hear it? Okay. Thought you would.

'English trio come down for short holiday break. Unknown to them their father's killer has been released from prison. He is full of hatred and wants revenge on English sisters whose evidence put him away. Breaks into house. Terrible struggle. He kills one of the English sisters and her husband. Second sister comes up behind him and brains him with a large rock. Terrific, isn't it? Such suspense! Such elegance!

'But wait, our story isn't over. You ask yourself the crucial question. How was the younger sister killed? And the answer is . . . LIKE THIS!'

172

There was a terrible blow on the door as though Flora had hit it with a hammer.

'And this!'

The door shook again.

'And this! And this!'

The cool, mocking tone had gone. She seemed gripped by hysteria.

Jo remembered the lighter in her pocket and flicked it on just as Flora hit the door again. She saw the tip of an axe break through the panelling of the door. Wood splinters were embedded in the panda's fur.

Flora stopped and Jo could imagine her standing outside trying to catch her breath for the next onslaught.

If she succeeded in making a hole large enough for her hand she could easily reach in and work the lock as well as the bolt.

Even as Jo was considering this, Flora attacked the door again. It was a simple inexpensive pine door consisting of four thin panels in a wooden frame.

Now the blows had less of the hammer-like quality, more of the sound of wood tearing and splitting.

There was a pause. Jo thought she heard a different noise. She flicked on the lighter. Flora's hand was already on the lock, turning back the nurled knob. She held the lighter to Flora's fingers. There was a scream and the hand was jerked back.

Silence. A kind of choking noise, either rage or pain. Then Flora's voice.

'So you are there!'

'Yes. I'm here.'

'I'd forgotten about the lighter.' She laughed. It was a strange unamused sound. 'Don't go away.' A rain of blows came at the second panel. Anger and pain, madness, had given her strength, for after half a dozen, she had broken through.

Jo dropped the panda and waited. She wanted both

hands free. Light was streaming through the holes giving her enough to see by. And the first thing she saw was the long kitchen knife with which she had tried to open the coffee mill. Flora swung it in a vicious arc. It became a silver streak in the semi-darkness.

Jo leapt out of reach, but in doing so, became entangled with the panda and fell heavily backwards against the rear wall of the toy cupboard. There was a splintering, tearing noise as her body broke through the flimsy false wall made of hardboard and covered in wall-paper. The smell of lavender was overwhelming.

She fell partly on to what seemed to be a bed of it, all neatly dried and stacked. She pulled herself up and found herself in a dark space somewhat bigger than the cupboard, but basically the same shape.

The first thing she saw was a shotgun leaning against the wall. Then the light suddenly brightened as Flora switched on the one in the cupboard. It lit up the thing that lay on the bed of dry lavender, the thing in the flowered dress and stockings and shoes and what looked like a wig but wasn't.

Flora stood in the toy cupboard doorway. Light glinted on the knife blade.

Dubois had driven the four kilometres to Cogolin angry at himself but even more angry at Drac. This was turning into a night of it. When it had begun he had thought it would go quickly and easily: sit outside La Corniche, wait for Drac to start his car, then arrest him. He had not envisaged this.

There were few bars in Cogolin and he had driven past each one. Drac's car was not visible. Dubois would have bet that Drac would have continued drinking. If not, then he must have gone back to his house. Maybe he had liquor there.

In that case, Dubois would have to pay him a little visit.

And the English too. He'd have to tell them. Drac playing with the dog outside his cottage was one thing, a drunken Drac roaming the countryside was quite another.

And you never knew, this might turn out well. He'd show the English that he was a responsible local cop looking after the interests of foreigners.

He put his foot down and was soon turning on to the Route du Canadel. He saw Drac running up the road. He only saw him for a second then he vanished.

He braked and stared into the trees. He had no wish to follow Drac into such a thicket, yet what was he to do?

He pulled out his gun and checked the magazine. Gingerly he got out of the car. He had left the lights pointing at the thicket.

'I'll give you five seconds to come out with your hands up,' he said. He wasn't sure what he was going to do after five seconds but, he told himself, at least he was doing his duty.

A figure rose almost at his feet and his heart felt it was dropping into his bowels. But it was not Drac. It was the man he had seen at the house earlier. The lover of the sister.

'For God's sake, don't shoot,' Roger said.

'What are you playing at?' Dubois said, angry at having been frightened.

'You're the cop who came to the house, yes?'

'Of course.'

'Christ, you people are quick. I've only just phoned.'

'Phoned?'

'I'll tell you as we go.' He climbed into Dubois' car.

'Go? Go where?'

'The Fleming house. There's something going on.'

'Oh Jesus. Drac!'

175

21

'So,' Flora said. 'You found her.'

'Found who?' Jo said.

'Who do you think?'

'Oh my God!' She felt the bile come up into her throat. That mass of hair and bones, that flowered dress, those shoes . . . 'Oh dear God!' She swallowed her own vomit and then felt her eyes fill with tears. 'It can't be! I don't believe it!'

But she did believe it.

'Who did you think it was then?' Flora said, her voice neutral.

'I don't know. I . . . Flora . . . Please Flora. Who . . . ? Did father . . . ?'

'Do it? He was an accessory after the fact. I think that's the phrase.'

'You mean it was . . . ? It was YOU!'

Under the glowing eyes, Flora's face seemed almost that of a stranger. In some peculiar way the structure had changed so that Jo only half recognised her as her sister. Her coat hung open almost hiding the knife but each time she moved it glinted.

'Don't shout. Yes, sweetie, it was me. Don't you remember? No of course you don't. You were too small. She was treating him badly. Drinking. Shouting at him. Making his life a misery. They fought all the time. He couldn't work. He told me we would have to sell the house. Go back to England. I'd have to go to boarding school. I didn't want that.

'I was happy here, the happiest I've ever been.' Her voice softened. 'I was close to father. So close he even used to read me his plays as he was writing them. To me! Not to mother. She was spoiling everything. Don't you see that?'

'And so . . . so . . . '

'So I decided it was best to . . . well, to remove her. Best for her too. She wouldn't have lasted more than a few years. She was miserable. She hated France. There was nothing for her to do. So she drank.'

Into Jo's mind flashed the letter from Marie-Claire to Roger. She had hated London.

'So I gave her something to drink. One of those garden things. She was so drunk she couldn't tell.'

'So the drowning— '

'That was father's idea. He didn't want anything to happen to me, you see. He faked the drowning and put her in here. It was easy enough. The cupboard was so big he was able to block up half of it. He did everything beautifully. Even to the lavender. That was his idea. I don't have to elaborate, do I?'

'And that's why he . . . why he made us change rooms?'

'That's right, sweetie.'

Flora came a step further. Jo grabbed the shotgun and pointed it at her.

'Don't be silly. It's not loaded.'

'How do you know?'

'Because I put it there.'

'This is father's gun, isn't it?'

'That's right, sweetie.'

'But why put it in here?'

Little Miss Muffet . . .

'Flora . . . did you . . . you . . . ? Oh my God! FLORA!'

'Well, it wasn't my fault. I mean, we'd been so close. And after mother died, we seemed even closer. He knew

177

how much I loved him, you see. I remember him saying he didn't want me out of his sight. That's how close we were.

'But then she came along. The bloody tart from next door.'

Jo was in a kind of dream, a nightmare. She seemed to be standing outside herself, watching. It was the only way she could regain her self-control. By telling herself that this *was* a dream.

'So because you couldn't have him to yourself, or you thought he was being unfaithful to you, or whatever, you killed them both!'

'They were like animals! Grunting and pawing! What else could I do? And Drac was there. I saw him watching. That's what made it possible.'

'And you made me think . . . You put it in my mind . . . Even little Joanna was a witness. Only it was to something that never happened.'

'Something like that. Have you ever seen those drawings where the artist leaves the nose unfinished or just puts in a small line for the jaw? The eye fills in the other lines. It's odd how the human mind fills in the gaps too. So often we don't see things. We only think we do. Now give me the gun.'

'When did you put it in here?'

'Years later. I opened up the wall and put it in and then re-papered the whole room. Don't you think that was clever – I mean doing it all myself?'

'And before that?'

'It was in the boiler room where it had always lived. They never even bothered with it. The police, I mean. Drac was so obvious. He'd had this feud with father about the wall and about the land. And he was always climbing into our garden and shooting things just to show he was not going to give in to an Englishman.

'They did a test on his hands. It's called a paraffin

test. I read about it. It proves that a person actually fired a gun. And he had fired it that morning. And then there was my word and your word and the body of his naked wife. Why on earth would the police look anywhere else? Give me the gun.'

'Why did you hide it then?'

'Well, I grew up. I could do things I couldn't do when I was young. Like pry the hardboard away and replace it and re-paper. So a couple of years ago I thought, why not? Why leave any loose ends? Why not make things tidy?'

'You were always the tidy one, weren't you? I was surprised at the empty vodka bottles.'

'Oh, that was Mike. I asked him to put them out. But you know how he is.'

'When did you . . . When did he . . . ?'

'Not too long after you were married.'

'That was nice, a nice sisterly act.'

'You were another one who tried to take father. It was only fair.'

Jo had spun though a succession of emotions: horror, fear, humiliation, now anger. But she had to remain cool. Flora was cool, the coolness of the psychotic. Somehow she must match that.

'Give me the gun, Jo. It's not loaded, believe me.'

'But that's the point,' Jo said. 'I don't believe you. Remember what you were saying about filling in the spaces? Are you quite sure one of your husbands or one of your boyfriends, didn't pick up the gun, load it, and go out for a morning's shooting?

'You couldn't have been here all the time. You must have gone shopping. You must have had your hair done in St Tropez. Think, Flora, of all the things that could have happened. It's just like when we were at school and father thought it was safe to have a little pre-prandial fornication.'

179

'Shut up!'

'You see?'

'Don't talk about it that way!'

'But it's true. The moment your back was turned he was after the first thing he could lay his hands on. That's why you shot him. You couldn't bear it. So you see we not only think we see things; we think we know things. The gun may be loaded.'

She saw the blankness drain from Flora's eyes to be replaced by doubt and indecision.

Jo said, 'A very boring boyfriend of mine once showed me how to shoot one of these. There's something called a safety catch. This must be it.'

'I'm telling you! The gun's not loaded!'

'Do you push it forward for off? I can't remember. So I'll push it forward.'

She advanced a step and Flora backed into the room.

'If I remember, you put your finger here. That's on the front trigger – but you'll know all this anyway – and it'll fire one of the barrels.'

'You little bitch! Do you really think you can frighten me?' Flora leapt at her.

Jo was flattened against the wall. Flora still had the knife in her hand, the other hand was forcing the barrel of the gun upwards. Jo fought but Flora had the strength of a steel cable.

Her face was inches from Jo's. Her eyes were huge and glowed like coal. Jo felt the strength begin to go in her arms. In desperation she pulled the triggers.

There was only a double click as the firing pins struck empty chambers. Flora stepped back. 'You see, sweetie? I told you.'

Jo flung the shotgun at her and ran from the room. At the head of the stairs she heard Flora's laugh.

'Run!' Flora shouted. 'Run! I also told you I'd locked up.'

Jo went down the stairs in twos and threes, bounding past the dead body of Mike. Something caught the corner of her eye in the semi-darkness. Just a shadow. But she was past and scrabbling at the front door. The key was missing.

She turned.

Flora was at the bottom of the stairs, the knife in her hand.

'Now will you believe me?' she said, triumphantly.

And then the shadow materialised. Drac had pulled himself up by the side of the staircase. His face and shoulders were covered in blood, his eyebrows encrusted with it. As Flora came past him he gripped her arm. She screamed. Using the last of his strength he hauled her bodily over the banister rail and locked his hands around her throat. He groaned with rage and pain. Flora fought him like a tigress. Again and again she drove the knife into his belly.

But it was too late. Twenty years of hatred gave him additional strength. Flora made a gurgling, gasping sound. Then there was a crack of a bone shattering and both bodies toppled to the floor.

Even as they fell, the front door burst open and Dubois and Roger Maillet ran into the room.

'Oh, Jesus Christ save us!' Dubois said, expressing both their thoughts.

More than thirty kilometres away, on a small winding road, near La Garde Freinet, Willi pulled up behind a silver Saab parked on the grass verge. It had British plates. Willi was confused, tired, angry, lost and extremely sorry for himself.

Two men stood at the side of the Saab. Neither looked English but Willi was no expert on the English.

'Shall we take his petrol?' Figeras said as they watched Willi approach.

'Why not take the car?' Espino said, and took out Roger's pistol.

Willi reached them. *'Excusez moi . . .'* he began. Then his brain told him, no, no, they were English. 'Excuse me please,' he began again. 'I am lost. I wish to go to La Motte . . .'

At this point Espino pushed the gun in Willi's face. He opened the Saab's door. 'Get in,' he said.

He was speaking a patois and Willi had little idea what he was saying but he did not need a translator.

He got in.

Figeras brought up the other car. 'Ready?'

'Ready,' Espino said and, with the pistol, whacked Willi on the side of his natty Tyrolean hat.

The two gypsies drove off into the night.

'You think they'll believe his story when he wakes up?' Figeras said.

'Who cares? Bloody English *rosbif*!'

22

Jo Townsend, a mug of steaming coffee in her hand, stood in the early spring sunshine on the balcony of a top floor apartment in London's Eccleston Square and looked out over the plane trees just coming into leaf. This rented flat was her home now.

Nothing in it belonged to her. The beds, the curtains, the carpets, the reproduction antiques, were functional but impersonal. Renting it had been a conscious effort to cut herself off from her recent past. She hated it.

For the first time in her life she had enough money on the horizon not to have to worry. She owned two houses and one apartment and all would be sold as soon as the legal requirements had been fulfilled. She no longer had to wait by the phone for a part in a play. She did not have to think of how much she'd make on a wet Sunday at Camden Lock Market.

She was independent.

And yet what was the point in being independent if you had no one to share your independence? She knew that was muddled phraseology – if not also muddled thinking – but she knew what she meant.

And at what cost was she independent!

She was still on sleeping tablets and tranquillisers, she still had nightmares. She was still ambushed by sudden pictures flashing into her mind of scenes from the house that night.

Those events had been followed by days and weeks of

torture and she was not sure what she would have done had Roger not simply taken her over. He had removed her to a hotel in St Tropez, had been with her when the police and media had questioned her. Had stayed by her side while the whole story unfolded, had been involved himself when Figeras and Espino had been arrested.

Eventually all the pieces of the jig-saw began to fit, even the presence of Willi. That had come from the gypsies but of the man himself there had been no sign. She wished Willi had been caught, and he would remain in her mind for a long time.

But at last the questioning was over, even Dubois had stopped pestering her about the house.

'I don't know what I'm going to do,' she had said. 'But if I sell it I shall put it into the hands of an agent.' He had looked disappointed, but Roger had finally brushed him off.

When everything was wrapped up she had returned to London and Roger had gone to see his parents in Paris. Her mind had been occupied by the maze of detail that surrounded wills and intestate estates, and that had helped. Now everything had been signed that needed signing, everything discussed that needed discussing. She had been to lawyers and accountants and tax people and of course Scotland Yard.

The Drugs Squad had searched both the house in Pimlico and Flora's flat in Camden Town and had found half a dozen coffee mills. But no heroin. It was assumed that Mike and Flora had taken it all to France.

Then the police had picked up Harry Evans and he'd talked his head off. Poor Harry, she thought. She'd never even suspected he was a user.

Innocent, that's me. Roger had said: 'You're not very inquisitive.'

Maybe that was her trouble. Remembering that brought him back vividly. She had waited for him to get in touch with her, but it had been like waiting for a part in a play that never came. So she phoned Agence France Presse and found that from Paris he had been sent to Cambodia.

He could have phoned she thought. He might have written.

Well, to hell with him. Who needed men?

There was one task she still had to do and that was to go through papers. There were two tea chests full of Mike's and Flora's and her father's.

She shied away from Mike's and Flora's. She'd do those when she was stronger. Her father's first, then.

They were in several box files and she fetched a large black refuse bag and sat in the sun in the middle of the yellow carpet and looked at play contracts for 1956, royalty statements, letters from his agent. Nothing of any value.

Then, in the last file she came on the manuscript of a play. She looked at the title: *The Toy Cupboard*. She frowned. She had read all her father's plays.

She turned over the pages.

Little Miss Muffet . . .

It was like a throb in her brain and she felt a kind of sick dread steal over her. Even as she read the opening words she knew instinctively what was to come.

'A living-room in the Reddings' house in the South of France. It is an old Provençal farmhouse with a large fireplace. There is a sofa and chairs stage right. A staircase leads to the upper floor. The Reddings are at their luncheon.

'The family consists of four: two adults, George and Mary Redding, and two daughters, Valerie and Belinda. Valerie is thirteen, Belinda somewhat younger. As the luncheon proceeds we discover that Mary Redding is extremely drunk. The others try not to notice this . . .'

Fearfully she read on. There it was . . . the writer husband . . . the drunken wife . . . the intense father-fixated
daughter . . . the poisoning . . . the panic . . . the deci-
sion to bury the body deep in the walls of the house
itself . . . everything . . .

The sun went behind a dark cloud and the light drained
from the room. She felt herself in a state of feverish
anxiety. She did not want to read on but the pages
seemed to turn themselves. Even some of the dialogue
was that spoken by Flora that terrible night.

'He used to read his plays to me,' she had said with
insane pride.

It was all there . . . a template for murder . . .

The phone rang.

Jo came out of her trance with a cry. Her whole body
was shaking. She fumbled with the receiver, dropped it,
picked it up.

'Hello,' she said.

It was Roger. Just hearing his voice caused a huge dark
cloud to lift from her. She tried to visualise him phoning
from somewhere overlooking the Seine perhaps, or in the
very centre of the city.

Suddenly shy, she asked about the weather.

'Wonderful. And London?'

'Cold but sunny.'

'Really? I have spoken to my office. They tell me
it is raining there.'

'Nonsense.'

'I must be sure. Please make sure.'

'I am sure.'

'Then make certain.'

'Why do you— '

'I have a thing about weather.'

Carrying the phone she went to the window and looked
down into the street. The sun was shining again. The
branches of the trees waving in the wind. So was a figure

at the phone box on the corner. He had stepped out on to the pavement and was waving his arm violently.

'Roger!' she said out loud.

They had lunch in an Italian restaurant nearby. She told him everything that had happened since coming back. He told her about the refugee camps in Cambodia. The misery and suffering of the people had caused him to sink into a kind of limbo. Just to get his work done had been all he could manage. On top of that Marie-Claire was divorcing him. He had not been able to bring himself to write to Jo.

They stayed until the restaurant closed. Then she took him back for coffee.

'You're thinner,' she said.

'And you are no longer a schoolgirl.'

They went out in the last of the sunshine and walked by the river. He told her he was being transferred back to Paris. His parents were moving to Grasse. He was moving into their apartment on the Left Bank.

'It is large,' he said. 'It is also very beautiful. It looks out over the river. Really, it is too big for me.'

'Why don't you share?'

'Maybe. But it is difficult to get the right person.'

The sun was streaking the Thames with red. Battersea Park looked like a magic wood across the water.

'What would the right person have to be like?'

'She would have to be a woman. I do not like male company. That's why I don't join clubs. No, it has to be a woman. Beautiful. Intelligent. Warm. Someone who can organise. She must speak French. And she must want children.'

'That's quite a list. When are you going back?'

'It depends.'

'On what?'

'On whether she will come with me.'

They were on the middle of Battersea Bridge and the

traffic was building up as he turned and kissed her. She had not been kissed in the street, in a park or on a bridge for longer than she could remember.

They kissed for a long time.

The traffic lights turned red. A bus carrying a group of nuns stopped opposite them. They watched fascinated as Roger and Jo wound about each other.

At last they came apart. Jo saw her audience. She gave a slight bow. As one, the nuns enthusiastically clapped their hands.

If you have enjoyed this book and would like to receive details of other Walker Mystery-Suspense novels, please write for your free catalog:

Walker and Company
720 Fifth Avenue
New York NY 10010